A SECRET WEAVERS ANTHOLOGY

A Secret Weavers Anthology

Selections from the White Pine Press Secret Weavers Series: Writing By Latin American Women

Edited By
Andrea O'Reilly Herrera

WHITE PINE PRESS · FREDONIA, NEW YORK

Publication of this book was made possible, in part, by grants from
the National Endowment for the Arts
and the New York State Council on the Arts.

These are works of fiction. Names, characters, places, and incidents are
either the product of the author's imagination or are used fictitiously, and
any resemblence to actual persons, living or dead, or locales is purely coinci-
dental.

Book design: Elaine LaMattina

Cover painting: Heteo Perez

ISBN 1-877727-82-2

Secret Weavers Series, Volume 13

Printed and bound in the United States of America

10 9 8 7 6 5 4 3 2 1

White Pine Press
10 Village Square, Fredonia, NY 14063

Library of Congress Cataloging-in-Publication Data

A secret weavers anthology : selections from the White Pine Press Secret
weavers series, writing by Latin American women / edited by Andrea
O'Reilly Herrera.
p.   c.m — Secret wevers series ; v. 13
ISBN 1-877727-82-2 (alk. paper)
1. Spanish American literature—Women authors—Translations into English.
2. Spanish American literature—20th century—Translations into English. I.
O'Reilly Herrera, Andrea. II. Series.
PQ7087.E5S43   1998
860.8'09287'098—dc21   98-28606
                                                            CIP

A SECRET WEAVERS ANTHOLOGY

SECTION III — THE POLITICS OF DOMINATION

SECTION IV — WOMEN AND LANGUAGE

In memory
of our most extraordinary and beloved Adela,
con mucho cariño y el mas profundo amor.
1.14.98

PREFACE

White Pine Press created the Secret Weavers Series in 1987. Prior to the establishment of this series, English-speaking readers could read in translation only work that belonged to a select sector of Latin American literature, largely literature written by men of the Boom Era: Jorge Luis Borges, Julio Cortázar and Carlos Fuentes. The Secret Weavers Series filled an enormous void in the North American cultural and literary realm. At last the voices of Latin American women—which had been ignored by the large publishing houses—were given a space of their own in which to be heard.

The series began with the publication of a bilingual edition of poems by Alfonsina Storni, one of the most important feminist poets of the twentieth century. There followed a series of anthologies, among them the landmark collection *Landscapes of a New Land: Short Fiction by Latin American Women, Secret Weavers: Stories of the Fantastic by Women from Argentina and Chile, Pleasure in the Word: An Anthology of Erotic Writing by Latin American Women, What is Secret: Stories by Chilean Women,* and *A Necklace of Words: Short Fiction by Mexican Women.* Interspersed with these collections were books by single authors: *A Gabriela Mistral Reader,* which brought this Nobel Prize-winning author's prose work into English for the first time, along with a selection of poetry from all phases of her career; *The Lost Chronicles of Terra Firma,* a novel by Nicaraguan author Rosario Aguilar; *Ximena at the Crossroads,* a novel by Peruvian Laura Riesco; and *Happy Days, Uncle Sergio,* a remembrance of 1950s Puerto Rico by Magali García Ramis.

The purpose of establishing the series was not to create hierarchies or definitions of north and south but, rather, to open new doors and create multiple opportunities for Latin American women to establish themselves in U.S. literary culture and for North American readers to see themselves and their lives from the vantage point of their neighbors to the south.

From feminine voices which speak to us from that time when America was first discovered to those voices still seeking to define the "American" experience and voice, this anthology brings together the voices of women who wove their lives into their words and, in so doing, wrote a feminine history of the Americas.

My own relationship with White Pine Press began with the inception of the Secret Weavers Series. By 1987, I had begun to feel like a writer, but I wrote only in Spanish. Where could I find an audience

13

for my work in translation? Writer David Barsamian suggested I send
some of my work to Dennis Maloney, editor of White Pine Press, who,
as David said, was also a poet and had a keen interest in human rights.
After accepting a position at Wellesley College, I sent my poems to
Dennis and our literary collaboration was born. I believe that few writ-
ers and publishers have created so deep an alliance, and it is an alliance
not based on fame or fortune. What holds us together is a deep com-
mitment to bringing forth those voices traditionally overlooked by
U.S. publishers. The books in this series are truly works of love, and
the series continues to flourish. It is, without a doubt, one of the most
prestigious collections of Latin American women's literature pub-
lished in the English language.

It is our hope that by bringing forth these voices, we will incorpo-
rate in the reader's cultural imagination voices that possess extraordi-
narily lyrical and artistic resonance, voices with a political and social
conscience which will leave their mark and transfer the reader's
response into activism, a sense of social conscience, and tolerance.

I invite you to participate in the open, colorful and warm realm of
The Secret Weavers Series, where words are sometimes winged crea-
tures, whispered messages, clay vases and memories. All acts of writ-
ing imply a public dimension, a desire to be heard. I invite you to dia-
logue with these secret weavers from the most remote lands of
America and to share in the deep resonance of their words.

—Marjorie Agosin, Editor
Secret Weavers Series

INTRODUCTION

As the ancient story of Scheherazade suggests, women have always used language and storytelling not only as a means to survive, but as a way to preserve memory and make meaningful their experiences. Despite a few isolated examples, such as the seventeenth-century Mexican nun Sor Juana Ines de la Cruz and the nineteenth-century Cuban playwright, poet and novelist Gertrudis Gomez de Avellaneda, Latin American women have, until recently, been barred entrance not only to the public sphere, but to cultural circles, as well. Though Latin American[1] women have always "poeticized their experiences," as Marjorie Agosín observes, through the written and spoken word, few managed to establish themselves in the national and international literary world until the latter half of the twentieth century.[2] Though there are exceptions, such as Gabriela Mistral (Chile), Luisa Valenzuela (Argentina) and Elena Poniatowska (Mexico), it wasn't until the 1970s that Latin American women's writing attracted significant critical attention.

Several simultaneous developments, such as the emergence of authoritarian governments in many Latin American countries and the international Women's Consciousness Movement—which prompted a mounting social awareness among the general population—precipitated women's entrance into the national literary arena. During the late 1950s and throughout the 1960s, literature written by Latin American women tended to examine the relationship of their personal experiences within the domestic sphere not only to their respective patriarchal cultures, but to social and religious institutions in general.

As Margarite Fernández Olmos and Lizabeth Paravisini-Gebert point out, the 1970s, however, "mark a turning point" for female writers in Latin America. Not only does the work produced during this period reflect a heightened sense of political consciousness, but it reveals the impact of the international Women's Movement. As Fernández Olmos and Paravisini-Gebert note, during the 1970s Latin American women "began to receive long-overdue critical attention, and distinctions in their use of new [thematic, linguistic and narrative] approaches to express old enduring problems began to emerge: parody and humor to question the nature of power and expose the hypocrisy of traditional notions of gender roles."[3]

Although Latin American female writers have gradually gained notoriety in their respective countries, their work has, until recently, been largely neglected or overlooked by North American publishing houses. As Marjorie Agosín points out, the Secret Weavers Series was not only established to "fill an enormous void in the North American cultural and literary realm," but is dedicated to bringing the voices of Latin American women to a wide-ranging English-speaking audience. Employing a thematic, rather than a chronological, geographical, or specific historical framework, *The Secret Weavers Anthology* not only celebrates the tenth anniversary of the Series, but is designed to provide the teacher of Women's Studies and multiethnic literature with a diverse range of Latin American women's voices addressing a wide variety of topics.[4] Though it cannot hope to be all-inclusive, this collection features works from various volumes in the Series that represent the general theoretical positions and central debates and issues which appear in the writing of Latin American women. In the process, it expresses both the plurality and universality of the responses that Latin American women have articulated in regard to their positions as females, and to their societies in general.

Divided into four interwoven sections, the anthology opens with a series of short stories which create a kind of prismatic effect in that they all reflect in some way upon the constructed nature of personal identity as it relates to the overlapping themes of conformity, power, and language and the further intersections of gender, race, and class. "Regarding My Mestizo Self," the first story in the collection, raises fundamental questions regarding cultural identity. Written from a position of hybridity—the legacy of the Spanish Conquest—Marcela Guijosa's story simultaneously acknowledges the sense of "doubleness" or bifurcation that is intrinsic to the identity of the female post-colonial subject yet, at the same time, circumvents Gayatri Spivak's claim that the female subaltern cannot speak[5] or the position that there exists some essentialist core of identity which can be fully recuperated and distilled from the syncretic mix. In essence Guijosa's story, like Derek Walcott's seminal essay "The Muse of History," gives "strange and bitter and yet ennobling thanks" for the "monumental groaning and soldering of two great worlds." Although Guijosa acknowledges that the Mestiza is an equal mix of antithetical forces and characteristics, she suggests that these combating aspects of identity are, to borrow Walcott's words once again, "like the halves of a fruit seamed by its own bitter juice."[6]

Ana María Guiraldes' darkly comic "The Family Album," a story which recalls Gabriel García Márquez's "The Handsomest Drowned

Man in the World," portrays a widow (whose husband died unexpectedly) who goes to surprising lengths to keep up the appearance of a "dignified family" for the mourners attending her husband's wake. All nearly comes undone, however, when an acquaintance asks to see a photograph of the deceased "surrounded by his family," something which the widow does not possess. The family, being "the most basic and ancient social institution," as Ian Robertson observes, and, moreover, a fundamental social unit in most Latin American societies, functions as the keystone to Doña Adela's identity.[7] In response to the request, therefore, Doña Adela insists that her husband be taken from his casket for a photograph—a decision, she acknowledges, which is prompted by her desire to demonstrate her "understanding" of "the value of tradition" in a society that strictly advocates and posits as a norm a nuclear familial system, which is both middle-class and patriarchal. In effect, Doña Adela is more concerned with appearing to conform to the public norm—as witnessed by her upset over the tear in her sofa and the possibility that she might run out of coffee—than distressed by the loss of her husband. Guiraldes undermines the image of the family that Doña Adela perpetuates and seeks to preserve, coupled with the elitist and sexist social "traditions" which undergird it, through the metaphor of the photograph—the object, Roland Barthes reminds us, that "gives itself out as complete" but ultimately "evades us." As Barthes observes, the photograph is a signification, a connotation, an "institutional activity" whose cultural or societal function is, purportedly, to "integrate" and reassure"; it, however, is "pure contingency," as the smile on Don Elias' face suggests, and, therefore, "outside of meaning" and "without relation to its essence."[8] In addition, the reader is repeatedly reminded of the fact that death is the great leveler, for it diminishes and nullifies the signicance of social values, distinctions and practices; Guiraldes comically punctuates the narrative with references to Doña Adela's husband, who remains peacefully unaware of the commotion around him and has "no intention of assuming a more elegant pose" while he is being photographed with his family.

Like Guiraldes, Ana Vásquez also takes up the dual themes of conformity and social identity and demonstrates the manner in which women's roles are caught up in the matrix of class and power. In "Elegance" she depicts a heroine who, having been denied the opportunity to pursue her studies, "cultivates the image of a mocking intellectual" in an attempt to transcend her working-class status. While riding in a taxi on her way to a party her boss has invited her to, the narrator—after having agonized over what she should wear—imagines that she has made the wrong decision. That Vásquez's narrator remains nameless suggests her social anonymity—both as a female and as a member of the working class—and her lack of identity. In her story, the author raises disturbing questions regarding the realities and fictions of development offered not only to women in general, but to Latin American women in particular, for the heroine, in an attempt to "fit in" with her colleagues and conform to their expectations, consciously models herself upon, and identifies with, stereotypical paradigms and icons drawn from Western popular culture: the Cinderella myth—a paradigm which suggests that the pinnacle of female success and happiness is marriage, both of which are dependent upon male prerogative—and the Chicana actress Rita Hayworth's signature role Gilda—the bombshell seductress, who exercises her power over men by exploiting her sexuality. Not only do these images suggest the degree to which Latin American women's identities have been shaped by Western notions of female sexuality and deportment, but they subtly allude to the extent to which they have been conditioned to accept the limited and oppressive maturation and behavior patterns offered to them both through fiction and through the media. Although Vásquez's heroine is conscious of the fact that her interior self does not correspond with what she perceives would be her accepted social self, she literally cannot imagine herself outside of the roles which, she fails to realize, are ultimately debilitating and self-diminishing.

Examining the role of the social outsider from a different perspective, Marta Jara's "The Englishwoman" is a retrospective in which the female narrator, who comes from a wealthy family, recalls with great regret her unkind treatment of her English nanny. Unlike the narrator in "Elegance," who merely registers the irony of the fact that as a child she had joined in with her classmates to ridicule and thereby alienate others who, like herself, sought to "fit in," the child's resistance to difference—summed up in her refusal to learn English—is out of ignorance, rather than malice. As an adult, Jara's narrator acknowledges her cruelty and, in the process, comes to the realization that despite the fact that the Englishwoman was unstylish and unattractive according to her standards, she was an "unfortunate" soul, isolated and anonymous in a society where no one could literally and figuratively comprehend her. In spite of the cultural and linguistic barriers that separate them, the narrator realizes that she and the nanny were bound together through their shared humanity.

The excerpt from Laura Riesco's novel *Ximena at the Crossroads* illustrates the manner in which women who defied the norms for accepted female behavior were stigmatized and ostracized. Riesco's adaptation of the *Bildungsroman* charts the growing sexual and social consciousness of Ximena as she is socialized into not only a gender role but into a mode of deportment deemed appropriate for her upper-class status. Ximena is characterized throughout the novel as an imaginative and fanciful romantic, who tells stories like "Scheherazade." In this particular episode her mother's cousin, Alejandra, and her female lover, who are themselves women who have defied accepted norms, request to see a photograph of the former's "Crazy Grandmother," a woman who "could not be tamed" and, unlike Doña Adela and Vásquez's anonymous narrator, "threw away all regard for proper manners and family reputation in provincial society, in order to live as she pleased." As a result of her willfulness, the grandmother was "excluded" from polite society and was eventually confined, like Sandra Gilbert and Susan Gubar's "madwoman in the attic," to a room in the *hacienda*.9 The chapter from which this excerpt is drawn also features a character named the weaver, a woman who has been "condemned" by society because she and her two illegitimate children live "in sin" with a man to whom she is not married. Ximena's exposure to these women and their illicit behavior and relationships awakens the child to the notion that hers is an intractable and close-minded society that not only refuses to tolerate, but punishes those non-conformists who consciously choose to be different.

The remaining works in section one either focus upon the notion that all human institutions and systems are constructed and, consequently, transitory and impermanent, or suggest the possibility that human beings are capable of transcending the physical and intellectual limitations of the material world or the social boundaries that divide them. The three poems by Alfonsina Storni, for example, draw a juxtaposition between the natural and the human worlds; through the topography of her poems, she reduces and diminishes not only human existence but human endeavor as well. Though Storni continued to develop certain themes throughout her oeuvre, in these poems nature represents an order that transcends the world of men, as opposed to a subjective, highly personal expression of her emotions and feminist concerns, as seen in her earlier works. Functioning as a kind of objective correlative for her disillusion with progress and human accomplishment and, as Marion Freeman suggests, the "dehumanizing effect" that the city has "on the individual spirit," the image of the city appears throughout Storni's later works.[10] In "Men in the City" the activities of men, "moving from one side to the other" in the city, are "suffocated" and "lost," made "almost invisible" in the twilight that "burns" on the horizon. In the same vein, the narrator in "Night" welcomes the veil of darkness that cloaks the "dirtiness of the streets." Reminiscent of T. S. Eliot's *The Wasteland* and Percy Shelley's "Ozymandias," "Litany for a Dead Earth" adopts a kind of post-Darwinian perspective. In her poem, Storni depicts a desolate earth that "support[s]" the "ruins and rubbish" of the cities, an image akin to the heaps of broken images depicted in *The Wasteland*. Moreover, by paralleling, for example, the great palaces of Spain with the huts of the Bedouins, Storni suggests that as the earth evolves and nature asserts herself, the barriers that human beings erect to differentiate from, and hold power over, one another will be "dissolved." Unlike Eliot's poem, the people of the earth try in vain "to reach the red rays" that the rekindled sun pours forth "because of some nameless mercy," for the "mud" that is "piled over their bones will be too thick." In the closing lines, however, Storni simultaneously rejoices in the human capacity for love and mourns the fact that no one will be left to cry "I love."

Section one draws to a close on a more hopeful note, for Torres and Ferré's poems and Mistral, Gallardo, and Rendic's stories emphasize the kindness of the human spirit and humankind's ability to survive and transcend. Celebrating the human capacity to hope and dream, Anabel Torres' "A Small Miracle" depicts a working-class woman who, unlike the narrator in Ana Vásquez's "Elegance," imaginatively envisions herself escaping the sordid reality of her life. In the same vein, Gabriela Mistral's "The Lark" invokes an image frequently utilized by the British Romantic poets: the lark. In her narrative, Mistral acknowledges the "burdens" of human life and the drudgery of habit, yet through the metaphor of the lark, she acknowledges the loftiness of human aspiration and imagination.

Among the final works featured in this section are those that employ either surreal or magical real elements to create what Michael

Dash calls a "counter-culture of the imagination."[11] Approaching the subject of human mortality from a slightly different angle than Ana María Guiraldes, Mistral poses the notion that only in death do we "achieve the vertical flight" and thereby escape the realities of material existence, which hold us back and bind us. Reminiscent of Gabriel García Márquez's "A Very Old Man with Enormous Wings," Sara Gallardo implements the marvelous or the fantastic in "The Man in the Araucaria," a short story that chronicles the activities of an insurance salesman who abandons his wife and family to pursue his dream. Disregarding the authorities, who attempt to prevent him from attaining his dream (the cautious, perhaps, who buy his insurance), the man dons his wings and "leav[es] the city at their feet"; though he eventually loses altitude, and thereby fails to realize his greatest aspirations, the man manages to defy at least some of the limitations that are placed upon him. Although some critics may stress the theme of paternal abandonment, as witnessed by the man's shirking of his responsibilities to home and family, one might, rather, focus upon the notion that Gallardo, like Mistral, employs flight as a metaphor for human aspiration and, like Storni, the city—with its religious and colonial monuments—as a symbol of human endeavor. Despite the fact that her story operates in a very particular historical, political and social context, Gallardo, through the use of the fantastic, joins the ranks of the great Latin American Magical Realists (such as Jorge Luis Borges, Gabriel García Márquez, Alejo Carpentier and Isabel Allende, to name but a few) and thereby "resists classification" and breaks with literary convention as defined by Western notions of genre. In so doing, Gallardo also posits, albeit through language and imagination, the unthinkable and the impossible, the "forbidden and the marginal" for, as Marjorie Agosín observes, "by talking and writing about the forbidden, about zones of silence, fantastic literature resides in the area of the always possible."[12] Also reflecting women's attempts to choose experimental and alternative ways to formulate and articulate their oppression and their desire to escape is Dora Alonso's "Cage Number One"; unlike Gallardo's story, however, Alonso's work seems to make a somewhat pessimistic statement regarding the possibility of transcending oppressive sociopolitical structures of authority, particularly as they relate to the experiences of women's everyday lives.

Countering Marta Jara's notion that "children cause suffering without knowing it," Amalia Rendic depicts a relationship between a boy and a dog, which ultimately brings out the very best in the adults around them. In "A Boy, A Dog, the Night" a machinist, Juan Labra, who works for a North American mining company, is asked to care for his *gringo* supervisor Mr. Davies' expensive and "elegant" show dog. (Mr. Davies, like Jara's Englishwoman, leads a lonely existence in a foreign land.) Soon after his departure, Juan's son, little Juan, develops a bond of love and communication with the dog that cannot be broken, even after its master returns. (By no mere coincidence, the dog's name is Black—a word which signifies the absence of color.) Not only does Rendic's story subtly suggest that racism and classism is a product of socialization and acculturation, but the conclusion demonstrates the human capacity for kindness and the possibility of transcending the social and cultural barriers that divide and separate the Labras and Mr. Davies.

The concluding work in section one, Rosario Ferré's "You Have Lost, They Tell Me, Your Reason," defends and advocates difference and nonconformity. In her poem, Ferré acknowledges the reality that those who consciously go against the grain are, like the "Crazy Grandmother" in Laura Riesco's novel, stigmatized and characterized as being something less than rational. Encouraging determination and courage, Ferré invokes Classical, archetypal images—such as Odysseus tied to the mast—of those who have "hardened their hearts" and closed their ears to society's judgments and criticism in order to pursue their separate visions.

* * *

Section two features works that consider women's prescribed roles in society—from maidenhood to motherhood—as they relate to the themes of gender construction and the relations between the sexes. Clearly, Latin American women's feminist writing is neither "singular" nor "monolithic," however, it is possible to trace a coherence in regard to their responses to their positions and roles in societies that have "traditionally been the most restrictive regarding appropriate social roles for women" and in which "machismo is still very much the norm."[13] The opening work in this section—Anabel Torres' poem "These are the Sweet Girls"—depicts the ideal of passive submissiveness, modesty and self-effacement to which "good women" were meant to aspire. Torres' poem is paralleled in the collection by an excerpt from Magali García Ramis' coming of age novel *Happy Days, Uncle Sergio*. Although García Ramis interweaves her feminist and political concerns throughout her work—by paralleling sexual and familial domination with Puerto Rico's dependent and subservient colonial status—this particular passage reveals the manner in which the middle-class female narrator is socialized into accepting traditional sexual, behavioral, and gender roles. Moreover, through the character of the deeply religious matriarch, Mama Sara, the author exposes a central fallacy regarding what has almost become a kind of stereotype of Latina maternity: although Latin women maintain indisputable authority within the domestic sphere and are, theoretically, revered for their ability to provide (legitimate) offspring, ultimately their power is restricted to this realm and, in the long run, they perpetuate the very systems and ideologies which oppress them.

Approaching the subject of motherhood from a different perspective, Marta Blanco's stream-of-consciousness monologue "Maternity" takes up a theme that characterizes the writing of many Latin American women: the sense of alienation and powerlessness women experience in their quest to maintain integrity and individual identity and control their personal relationships. Blanco's work portrays the fate of a disillusioned, pregnant narrator who, having been conditioned to believe that the childless woman is somehow "incomplete" and the crown of female "happiness" is maternity, has been abandoned by her lover; as a result, the woman undergoes an abortion. In the process of defying the accepted patterns of female sexual behavior, she has not only lost control over her body but lost her sanity as well. Adopting a slightly different trajectory, Cristina Pacheco and Giovanna Pollarolo depict the disillusion and dissatisfaction of married working- and upper-class women (respectively) who have attained what society deems as "happiness." "Noodle Soup" depicts the unromantic reality that a mother and her young daughter face in their struggle to survive both as a family and as individual women; in effect, Pacheco punctures the romantic myth (embodied in Marta Blanco's story by Western pop culture figures such as Bogart and Clark Gable) that "love" conquers all; on the other hand, "When We Meet Again" reveals that money, marriage and children fail to guarantee fulfillment and "happiness."

Adopting the same narrative strategy employed by Marta Blanco, Elena Poniatowska's "Happiness" highlights a theme that reverberates throughout Latin American women's writing: the sense of solitude experienced by women who have become entangled in dependent relationships in which they have renounced their own identities and creative potential. Reminiscent of Charlotte Perkins Gilman's "The Yellow Wallpaper," Liliana Heker's "When Everything Shines" and Marta Brunet's "Solitude of Blood" also depict passively submissive heroines who, having been conditioned from childhood to accept their subservient connubial and heterosexual roles, undergo nervous breakdowns in response to their untenable circumstances. In both stories the authors expose the monotony of domestic life and women's consequent obsession with the trivial, rather than the intellectual, cultural or the political.

Comparable to Alfonsina Storni's poem "You Want Me White," Heker's story reveals that the heroine, Daisy, has been conditioned to emulate the "white" and "radiant flower bud" after which she has been named—an image that Storni also invokes to signify the ideal of passionlessness and chastity to which women were expected to aspire, despite the obvious paradox when one considers the value placed on marriage and motherhood in these societies. Rather than portraying woman's empowering connection to the natural order (a theme often taken up by Eco-feminist writers and critics, which characterizes much of Storni's early works), both the poem and the short story suggest the negative and pejorative manner in which the feminine has been associated with nature. Incapable of envisioning herself as a separate individual, Daisy submits to madness and (presumably) "oblivion." On the other hand, the nameless Creole woman in Brunet's "Solitude of Blood" renounces passion when she submits to an arranged marriage with an older man whom her father has chosen for her. In effect, the woman's (literally and figuratively) sterile marriage—symbolized by the outfits she knits for other people's children—mirrors her relationship with her father. Compensating for her frustration and "humiliation," the woman comforts herself by invoking the image of a green-eyed boy she once knew as a young girl and derives her only pleasures from masturbating and from the music she plays on a phonograph she has purchased with her own savings. Drawing on an image employed by authors as seemingly disparate as Cristina García and Virginia Woolf, Brunet uses music to represent a transcendent order—an order which connotes the antithesis of the male realm of practicality and reason. Temporarily acting out her passions—behavior which is taken for madness by her husband and his business associate—the woman contemplates death as a means of escape from the loveless, "corrosive ardor" of her husband's lovemaking and her mechanical existence. However, upon being brought back to consciousness by a dog that has followed her into the fields she, unlike Heker's Daisy, opts for life at the conclusion, and thereby asserts her role as "the receptacle," to borrow Marjorie Agosín's words "of memory," passion, and happiness as she chooses to defy death and, consequently, "oblivion."

As Brunet's story suggests, Latin American women's passion and sexual expression has traditionally been repressed or veiled. In her preface to *Pleasure in the Word*, Marjorie Agosín points out that "eroticism, love and sensuality," like written language, "have been male preserves where intellectuals, historians, and sexologists wrote—and still write—about women's sexuality and eroticism, telling them how to think and feel."[15] Countering this reality, the remaining works featured in section two validate female potential and sexuality and passion, fecundity and maternity.

In her poem "My Stomach," Agosín defies the notion that beauty and happiness are dependent upon youth by taking on the persona of an elderly woman who rejoices in, rather than scorns or denigrates, her aging body. In the same vein, Rosario Castellanos' "Speaking of Gabriel" confirms the possibility that despite the discomforts of gestation and childbearing, children can enrich a woman's life and provide a defense against solitude. The second poem by Castellanos, "Origin," reveals the manner in which women began to transform and reinscribe fundamental patriarchal texts and ideologies as a result of the international Women's Consciousness Movement; like Ilke Brunhilde Laurito's "Genetrix" poems, Castellanos' poem reconstitutes the Genesis myth, which attributes woman's origins to man, and affirms the female's intrinsic and positive relationship to her natural surroundings. Written in the same spirit, Castellanos' poem "On the Edge of Pleasure" is a joyfully unbridled celebration of female eroticism and sexuality.

* * *

Though many of the works included in this anthology address issues such as the construction of the female self and the emancipation of the woman as an individual, rather than a gendered subject, all of the works featured in section three either focus on the authors' relationships to broader racial, ethnic, and national communities or reveal the extent to which Latin American women have used their writing to position themselves both within their larger communities and within specific historical contexts. In the 1970s, women all over Latin America visibly assumed an active role in promoting human rights. Section three, therefore, opens with several poems that aim to expose and protest the horrors that characterized the oppressive authoritarian political systems in Latin America. Poems like Emma Sepúlveda-Pulvirenti's "September 11, 1973" and "No" are overt polemics that clearly depict the condition of the politically powerless, as well as the terrors created by a tyrannical totalitarian regime; Marjorie Agosín's "The Most Unbelievable Part" exposes the sad reality that all human beings are capable of unspeakable violence and evil.

Though it ultimately suggests the inability to express the horrors of war and to enter what Agosín refers to as the "zones of pain," Idea Vilareño's "Maybe Then" stands as a testimony to the human will to survive and endure. In her poem, Vilareño not only allies herself with authors such as the French feminist writer Marguerite Duras (with her allusion to the latter's screenplay *Hiroshima, Mon Amour*), but she appeals to her lover with the hope that s/he is capable of the compassion and empathy necessary to even begin to broach the horrors that the narrator has witnessed and experienced. On the other hand, Romelia Alarcón de Folgar's "Irreverent Epistle to Jesus Christ" reveals the disillusion and bitterness of a people whose faith in a seemingly distant and "impassive" Christian God has failed to vindicate the senseless martyrdom of the "thousands of men" who have lost their lives in battle.

The following poems included in this section take up the related themes of absence and search, a trope which appears repeatedly throughout the writing of Latin American women. In these works, the authors frequently yoke together their personal, feminist, and/or political concerns. In Gabriela Mistral's "The Useless Vigil," the narrator waits in vain for a "disappeared" loved one who will never return; in the same vein, Marjorie Agosín's "Disappeared Woman I" simultaneously alludes to the nameless multitudes who were disappeared by the governments in Chile and Argentina and to the invisibility of women in these oppressive patriarchal cultures.

Several of the works included in this section take as their directive the exploration of the interconnection between the personal and the public. Seemingly conscious of the fact that the female body has, like language, been a common site of the struggle for political power, authors such as Teresa Calderon and Belkis Cuza Malé investigate and comment upon major historical events in their respective countries within the context of women's personal relationships and their activities within the domestic sphere. In works such as Calderon's "State of Siege" and "Domestic Battles," women's activities and experiences within the private arena and through their traditional roles—as wives and mothers—function as a microcosm of the larger historical or political scene. In these works, the poet draws a direct parallel between the private and/or domestic and the public political spheres by adopting military language to describe the relationship between the sexes. Although it acknowledges women's subordinate role to men and addresses the female's traditional exclusion from the public sphere where wars are waged and, as a result, history is made, Cuza Malé's "Women Don't Die on the Front Lines" figures the domestic sphere as a site of battle and the pregnant female as a soldier "on leave from the front." Approaching this topic from a different slant, Alaide Foppa personalizes the experience of war through her portrayal of a despairing mother. In her poem "Wound," a fearful mother anguishes over her ultimate inability to protect and "defend" her infant son.

Demonstrating women's increasing preoccupation with issues such as the definition of nation and nationhood, especially in a post-colonial context, poems like Blanca Wiethuchter's "Without Histories" represents an attempt to reclaim a cultural history which was denied or erased in the official records and master texts of Western history. A related subject which also appears in the writing of many of the authors gathered together in this section is the notion that Latin American women's exclusion from the main currents of economic and political life has essentially robbed them of historical significance and rendered them as ahistorical subjects. As Cuza Malé's "Women Don't Die on the Front Lines" suggests, women's subordination and their consequent restriction to the domestic sphere has relegated and reduced them (to borrow Edouard Glissant's vocabulary) to the "non-creative," "non-historical" periphery. Marjorie Agosin's work on the arpilleras or wallhangings (created by the mothers of Chile in memory of their disappeared), and the mothers of the Plaza de Mayo (who march every Thursday to protest the civil rights offenses witnessed in

Argentina), however, dramatically testifies to the fact that Latin American women have played a central role in tearing down the walls of silence and fear that have hemmed them in. Written out of a very specific political context, Gioconda Belli's "Nicaragua Water Fire" also seeks to redress this omission by elevating women's experience and endowing them with historical signfiicance. In her poem, Belli portrays women as active agents in the events that have shaped (a feminized) Nicaragua's identity. In addition to juxtaposing, and thereby endowing with equal significance, women's public and private activities—"the making of love, of bread, of children and of trenches"—Belli, defies a chronological reading of history by drawing parallels between the subjugation of women, the enslavement of the indigenous population by their colonial oppressors, and the tyranny of the Somoza regime.

Like Wiethüchter's "Without Histories," Rosario Aguilar's novel *The Lost Chronicles of Terra Firma* falls into a sub-genre of post-colonial literature which takes up the subjects of nationhood and history. Aiming to reclaim a "lost" colonial text, and thereby reinscribe the colonizer's account of the conquest of Nicaragua, Aguilar weaves together the dual themes of women's subordination and colonial oppression. In short, Aguilar's novel addresses Latin American women's "double oppression" (by nature of their gender and their post-colonial status) and represents an attempt to compensate for what Carole Boyce Davies and Elaine Savory identify as "the [historical] absence of a specifically female position on issues such as slavery, colonialism, decolonization, women's rights and more direct social and cultural issues."[14] By interweaving the narratives of several characters, most of whom are partial creations of the central female narrator's imagination, and adopting a narrative trajectory that unfolds history in a cyclical fashion, Aguilar simultaneously draws parallels between the condition of Nicaragua both before and after independence and links together the experiences of all women, regardless of their cultural affiliation, their race, or the period in which they lived. (That Aguilar's central narrator is a journalist is significant when one considers Latin American women's limited access to the media.) In the particular excerpt featured in this section, Aguilar not only focuses upon the isolation of a woman who is forced to live in exile, but she, like Marcela Guijosa, acknowledges the impossibility of "retracing one's footsteps" in an attempt to retrieve some essentialist historical or cultural truth or reality. As Doña Ana, the Indian, observes, "How is it possible...to separate that which has been united, or purify that which has already been mixed?" In addition, this passage reveals the violence and hypocrisy of the Spaniards, who sought to convert the Indians to Christianity but, ultimately, failed to "practice" what they "preached."

Carmen Naranjo's "The Compulsive Couple of the House on the Hill" also draws a direct analogy between women's social and sexual repression (as embodied by the wife who always walks two steps behind her husband) and the political context of oppression. In addition, Naranjo's story functions as a kind of double-barreled political parable and social critique which not only "overtly brings gender into the mix of power and politics," as Jeanette McVicker observes, but takes to task a society that allows itself to be wooed by political rhetoric and dominated by what Agosín describes as "the false ideologies of social charity."[15] Like Carpentier's *The Kingdom of This World*, Naranjos' story ultimately suggests that power corrupts and that all political systems are caught up in a matrix of greed, hypocrisy, and the lust for power.

Though most of the works presented in this section paint a dark portrait of the political realities facing many Latin American countries, section three closes on a more hopeful note with Clementina Suárez's "Poem for Mankind and Its Hope," a work that once again confirms the capacity of the human spirit not only to survive but to hope and dream as well.

* * *

The fourth section of the anthology gathers together works that focus exclusively upon women's relationship to language and the significance of appropriating the word in patriarchal societies where language and, more specifically, the literary text are the primary sites of an agonistic struggle for the possession of power and, as George Lamming suggests, the most potent instrument for cultural and social control and change.[16] The first two works featured in this section, Luisa Valenzuela's "Dirty Words" and Ángela Hernández's "How to Gather the Shadows of Flowers," acknowledge the manner in which the female writer—the woman who has appropriated patriarchy's "dirty," "filthy" words—has traditionally been feared and, therefore, stigmatized as being a madwoman and a witch. Unlike Audre Lord's claim that women ought not to use the master's tools to deconstruct his house and Salman Rushdie's insistence that the attempt to establish identity through a "fallen language" is fatal, Valenzuela charges female writers with the "arduous task" of reinscribing and reshaping the very words that men have implemented to repress them in order to "[transgress] the barriers of censorship" and "destroy the canons in search of an authentic voice."

In "Protest," Romelia Alarcoñ de Folgar expresses the notion that poetry is "defenseless" and "useless" in a world "of daggers" and "machine guns" where "there are unburied men abandoned in the streets": others, however, such as Alfonsina Storni, Cristina Peri Rossi, Delmira Agustini, Idea Vilareño, Clementina Suárez, and Julia de Burgos confirm the sustaining and curative power of poetry and the power of language to express the unspeakable and, therefore, unearth "the horrors of the void" and transform the impossible into reality. Expressing a notion akin to William Blake's concept of "a world in a grain of sand," Nancy Morejón ("Requiem for the Left Hand") suggests that by using the imagination to transcend the social and political boundaries that divide human beings, "all history can fit" in "the smallest map drawn on notebook paper."

Several of the poems included in this final section such as Suárez's and Cecilia Vicuña's, also stress the interactive relationship between the poem and its reader. Many acknowledge the vibrancy that is contained in the shell of language—the soul as it were—and though "each word," like John Keats' Grecian urn, may await "the traveler" in silence, each continues to sing. Others consider language and writing from a post-modern perspective. Alejandra Pizarnick, for example, in her poem "In This Night, In This World," and Ángela Hernández acknowledge the limitations and ultimate failure or "absence" of language the moment that it is "castrated" by the tongue or inscribed, and thereby frozen, "into a statue" of words to borrow de Burgos' image; nevertheless, as Agustini and Storni suggest, writers who are "blinded" by the "fierce and branding iron" are compelled to write in an attempt to express that which words can never capture, despite the notion that once committed to paper, inspiration, as Percy Shelley observed, fades like a coal that has begun to burn out.

In their attempt to image women's relationship to language, many of the writers included in this section liken inspiration, which is fleeting and can come at any time as Nancy Morejón suggests, to objects in the natural world and parallel the act of writing to coition and childbearing. In effect, as this collection suggests, Latin American women have forged a kind of new maternity which elevates women's experiences, especially in regard to their relationship to the natural world. As a result, they have subverted, recodified and deconstructed the logocentric master narratives both of Western culture and of their own respective patriarchal cultures. Although, as José Rabasa reminds us, all "cultural products should be taken as rhetorical artifices," by imitating, assimilating, internalizing and reinventing the word, Latin American women have valorized and validated their voices and, in the process, revised and transformed what we understand literature and writing to be.[17] In responding to what Cristina Peri Rossi calls their other selves—"the woman who dances in [their] ear[s]" and whispers to them of "ancient things"—they are fulfilling their roles as the "keepers," to borrow Valenzuela's words, "of textuality and texture."

—Andrea O'Reilly Herrera

1. I am adopting Agosín, Paravisini-Gebert, and Fernández Olmos' usage of the tag "Latin American" to include the women of South America, the Spanish Caribbean, Central America and Mexico.

2. See the introduction of *Landscapes of a New Land* (Fredonia, NY: White Pine Press, 1989) 1.

3. See the introduction of *Pleasure in the Word, Erotic Writing by Latin American Women* (Fredonia, NY: White Pine Press, 1993) 25-26.

4. Although time and space do not allow for the analysis of the specific historical contexts out of which the female authors represented in this anthology write, I am well aware of the dangers Chandra Talpade Mohanty points out in regard to treating the "Third World Woman" as "a singular monolithic subject" in an attempt to compensate for "the overwhelming silence about the experiences of women in these countries." See Talpade Mohanty's essay "Under Western Eyes, Feminist Scholarship and Colonial Discourses." *Boundary 2*. 12 (3), 13 (1) (Spring/Fall), 1984: 338-58.

5. "Can the Subaltern Speak?: Speculations on Widow Sacrifice." *Wedge* 7 (8) (Winter/Spring): 120-30.

6. See Walcott's essay in Orde Coombes' (ed.) *Is Massa Day Dead? Black Moods in the Caribbean* (New York: Doubleday, 1974).

7. See Chapter 24 of Robertson's textbook.*Sociology* (New York: Worth, 1977).

8. *Camera Lucida* (New York: Hill & Wang, 1982)

9. *The Madwoman in the Attic, The Woman Writer and the Nineteenth-Century Literary Imagination* (New Haven: Yale, 1979)..

10. See "Alfonsina Storni: An Introduction" in *Alfonsina Storni, Selected Poems* (Fredonia, NY: White Pine Press, 1987) iv.

11. "Marvelous Realism: The Way Out of Negritude." *Caribbean Studies.* 13 (4), 1974: 57-70.

12. See "Reflections on the Fantastic" in *Secret Weavers: Stories of the Fantastic by Women of Argentina and Chile* (Fredonia, N Y: White Pine Press, 1992) 1.

13. See Margarite Fernández Olmos and Lizabeth Paravisini-Gebert's introduction to *Pleasure in the Word.*

14. "Righting the Calabash: Writing History in the Female Francophone Narrative," *Out of the Kumbla.* Ed. Carole Boyce Davies and Elaine Savory [Fido] (Trenton, NJ: Africa World, 1990) 145.

15. See Agosín's introduction to *Landscapes of a New Land, Short Fiction by Latin American Women* (Fredonia, NY: White Pine Press, 1989) 4.

16. See "The Occasion for Speaking" in *The Pleasures of Exile* (London: Michael Joseph, 1960).

17. See *Inventing A-M-E-R-I-C-A: Spanish Historiography and the Formation of Eurocentrism* (Norman, Oklahoma: University of Oklahoma Press, 1993) 9.

SECTION I
IDENTITY AND DIFFERENCE

MARCELA GUIJOSA

REGARDING MY MESTIZA SELF

How easy it could have been. A pretty and complete blend. Like the story about the races: God puts little human figures in the oven, and some come out undercooked, and they're the white race. The better ones are dark, nice and golden, well done. Us.

As if God had kneaded Indian dough with Spanish dough, mixed them together into a single mass, then popped it in the oven. And the Mexican batch came out just right. All one shade, the color of coffee with cream.

If only the Spaniards had arrived, not killed anyone, and conversed with the Indians. If only they had agreed, and each Spanish man had paired up with an Indian woman, and vice-versa. Choose a girlfriend or boyfriend. Have children. Let's create a new race.

And if all of us had Spanish great-grandfathers and Indian great-grandmothers, and we remembered them fondly and venerated them equally, the two original, mythical races that gave us life, father of our flesh, mother of our flesh. If the two separate cultures lived on only in our memory, and our Mexican culture had preserved, and practiced daily the best of both worlds, now fused and kneaded and inseparable.

If only I weren't this poorly-made hodgepodge, with lumps of white flour and clumps of brown sugar that hurt me. If only I were all one color. If my dreams and my gods didn't tear me apart, tugging at me from shores separated by a vast sea of solitude.

If my pyramids were completely mine and if I understood the old language and the old rituals and the terrible plumed serpents and the skulls that watch me in a language I don't know.

If the cathedrals didn't weigh so heavily on me, stones shamelessly stolen from another religion. If I didn't carry such a heavy cross along ground strewn with cacti and entrails, my knees torn to shreds, my hands pierced by thorns, so as to see my Virgin of Guadalupe.

If I didn't have separate roots that threaten to split my trunk in two. If my feet weren't standing on such distant parcels of earth, my genitals sore and split, half over there, half over here, my womb open, my legs stretched at strange angles, always off balance.

Or my body and soul so far apart, so different, my flesh of this land, this water, and these volcanoes, yet my spirit so invaded by Latin words, and ballads, and Punic Wars and theological tomes.

If I only knew who I was without wearing a *huipil* and a *quesquémetl* one day, and a lovely silk or laced-edged piqué blouse the next, because after all, colorful embroidery and hand-loomed cotton belts are fine, but only if you're headed to Cuernavaca on a Saturday, or you work at the Colegio de México or the Museum of Anthropology, and they're having an *amusgo* or Guatemalan *huipil* contest. But underneath it all, you're a middle-class woman who can't afford the outfits you really like, certainly not clothes designed for wealthy, respectable people, or at least those considered respectable, linen suits and pure silk blouses, or blouses edged in lace like your grandmother used to make. And you're not a *tehuana* walking around in an embroidered top, long flowered skirt, and antique necklace because you live in Mexico City today, in the postmodern age, and when you show up in villages in native dress, the Indian women look down on you and even insult you for wearing clothes that aren't really your own. With your hair cut short, almost shaven, and your denim jeans, no matter how many San Pablito blouses and silver earrings you wear, you're half and half, a hybrid, split in two, a mermaid with the face of a woman, breasts, feminine arms and polished nails, and at the same time a blind, irrational, underwater animal, with cold and ancient blue-scaled flesh that smells of fish, unable to walk on land where you must live in order to survive, half air and half water, half sun and half shade, half cold and half warmth.

And so you are totally half and half, half Christian and half pagan and magical and idolatrous. Half masculine and half feminine, half free, active and brave, a conqueror, an adventurer, an evangelist, a teacher. Half night, moon, water and submission, dark and receptive, fecund, sleeping, cyclical. And crazy, and humid, and passive. Passive root, passive milk, passive tomb.

Translated by Nancy Abraham Hall.
From Volume 11: A Necklace of Words

Ana María Guiraldes

The Family Album

When Don Elias sighed his last breath, the newly widowed Mrs. Adela Lopez realized that she did not have time to cry. But her eldest daughter did cry, the three younger children cried and baby Thomas cried because it was his feeding time. In the midst of the sobs and whimpers, the doctor handed the widow the death certificate, which stated that Elias Jaramillo Valdebenito had departed this world at 10:40 a.m., victim of a cardiac arrest.

With handkerchief in hand just in case, the widow directed the preparations for the wake. And thus Don Elias, in his new three-piece suit with a pine-scented handkerchief in the breast pocket, was placed in the casket half an hour later. The four children obediently changed their clothes and washed their faces and hands before taking their places in the living room—a properly grieving but dignified family. The nanny held little Thomas, who had awakened in a bad temper that morning and was still crying.

Doña Adela, in her black suit and suede dress shoes, stood next to the casket looking at her dead husband and thinking that luckily there was enough coffee for the guests. The deceased, unaware of the commotion his death had caused, remained flat on his back, prepared for a long day of being contemplated.

The first visitors to arrive were three teachers—two women and a man. Neither they nor those who arrived later noticed the cleanliness of the house or the perfection of the children who were all lined up, secretly poking and pinching each other at the sight of Miss Zoila's beard and Miss Silvia's teeth. Nor did anyone admire the swiftness with which the housewife had prepared everything. They all knew that Doña Adela had managed to organize a Christmas party in a half hour and had collected shoes for poor children in a single morning, distributing them herself because she didn't trust anyone else. Even more reason, then, to expect her own husband's wake to be perfect. She was one of those women who never made a mistake or was caught off-guard. Until that day.

The two maids perspired as they hurried around the house under the commanding eyes of their boss. The cook opened the door for the guests, wiped the floor to erase the marks left by the professor's rubber soles and removed the empty coffee cups. The other maid, who was rather slow and easily frightened, walked Tommy around, shaking him whenever he kicked her, and fretted because the child wanted to look at his father sleeping in the big box and she didn't dare let him. The deceased man might wink at her, like he used to when he was alive, and then appear to her later in a cloud of smoke, wearing wings. The lady of the house went off to the kitchen several times to keep an eye on the preparations for lunch: the children weren't about to starve just because Elias had died. She even had enough presence of mind to give Samuel the gardener, who was charged with receiving the wreaths, a black tie and told him not to smoke because it was disrespectful.

All of this was done in consideration of the fact that Elias had died suddenly. If he had been ill a long time, she at least would have had time to mend the sofa so that the oldest daughter wouldn't have had to sit on the tear all morning to cover it up.

But no one is perfect. And so it happened that the music teacher, Miss Silvia, a piano and harp specialist, asked to see the family album. "I would so much like to see a picture of Don Elias surrounded by his family. He was such a solitary, hard-working man that I never had the pleasure of seeing him as the father of his family," she said in her sharp voice, her chest quivering.

Doña Adela, who was glowering at the little ones as they giggled at the drop of saliva that fell on Miss Silvia's lap when she pronounced the word "pleasure," stood there dumfounded. And since Miss Silvia spoke in the high-pitched voice she used in class, everyone heard her: "Yes, the family album, Doña Adela...Don Elias and all of his offspring, Doña Adela..."

And so Doña Adela, who never missed a detail, realized in the middle of her husband's wake that she didn't have a picture of the family.

And for good reason: Elias was a Rotarian, he ate out every week, he was president of whatever they asked him to be, a fireman, a friend to his friends.... In short, a thousand excuses tumbled out of the mouth of the distressed widow, who had the habit of examining what was done, not that which was not done.

While out of the corner of her eye she watched her eldest daughter wriggle around on the sofa, thus revealing the rip, she searched for a solution: a way of adorning the wall with a photo of poor Elias with the family he had managed to create with some effort and good humor, next to his wife, who had accompanied him through good times and bad, and perhaps next to the maids, who had served him during the last ten years (Doña Adela's maids stayed with her a long time). To show that hers was a family that understood the value of tra-dition and, most of all, so that no one could say that she, the widow of Jaramillo, had overlooked such an important detail, she decided to take her husband out of the casket. Without any crying or hysteria, as natural as could be. Besides, she would have done the same thing if she had discovered a scratch or some other defect in the casket. As she was giving Samuel (who had been smoking behind the rose bushes) clear instructions about getting the photographer, she noticed that Elias' face was beginning to look strange.

The teachers rose to the occasion. They immediately joined forces to help with the tasks at hand. Besides convincing the widow that it would not be necessary to open the drapes because the photographer always used a flash, they also informed her that luckily he was just returning from a neighboring farm, where he had taken pictures of a newly arrived family that wanted to be immortalized under the region's apple blos-soms and blue skies. The photographer, José Sotomayor, had been with the family for two days and had not heard about the recent death. Samuel, the odor of flowers and cigarettes still on his hands, had to do some talking to persuade him that Doña Adela needed a family picture because Elias was about to embark on a long journey (Samuel smiled a little as he said this), and that it would be good business because they would pay him double for the hurry. José was finally convinced.

When he arrived at the traveler's house, everything was ready. The entire family was waiting for him. In the place of honor, very rigid, shoulder to shoulder with his wife and the cook, stood Don Elias, impeccable in his blue suit. To either side were his children, wide-eyed and silent. The nanny, with Tommy asleep in her arms, wore the expression of having seen a ghost.

Doña Adela brusquely cut off the photographer's repeated requests for Don Elias to smile or raise his half-closed eyelids. And finally, clearly indignant, she told him to take the picture once and for all and that she didn't want to hear any more jokes about Elias looking exhausted from having been out all night. Reprimanded, the photographer said, "There, there, that's it, smile, sir," because Elias' jaw had fallen slightly. He had the wife step back a little to be in line with her husband, who had no intention of assuming a more elegant pose. The camera clicked and José excused himself to go to work in his studio.

And so, after some hustle and bustle in which everyone participated—retrieving the casket from the dining room and the wreaths from the pantry, returning to the foot of the casket the red carnations that Doña Adela had placed in a vase on the table to liven up the picture, giving the nanny a tranquilizer because she was sure the master had been staring at her, serving the children lunch and, of course, installing Don Elias in the same comfortable position he was in at 11:10 that morning—Doña Adela took her daughter's place on the sofa to receive the remaining guests who came to pay their respects. And finally, a couple of days later, with the first and last family picture hung on the wall, she went into her room to cry in peace and remember Elias, who smiled softly at her from the photograph.

Translated by Margaret Stanton.
From Volume 9: What Is Secret

Ana Vásquez

Elegance

PARIS, FRANCE

The black crepe or the blue silk? The silk one because it goes well
with the color of her eyes. But the cut of the skirt is no longer in style,
and besides, she doesn't have blue shoes. Then the black. She puts it
on decidedly and walks slowly to the mirror, smiling and greeting her-
self as if she were somebody else. But no, too long. She looks like a
nun dressed for Sunday Mass. She hikes it above her knees and turns
around to see the effect: a little shorter would be even better. She
shortens it hurriedly. Daniel said around ten o'clock; it's already 10:15
and she still has to iron it! But black looks good on her, it gives her a
dramatic look. And it hides the size of her hips, which are too wide.
The fabric is soft; she likes the way it drapes on her. It makes her feel
a little less anxious. Tonight it's absolutely necessary, indispensable,
that she look elegant so no one will think, not even for a second, that
she's just an office secretary.

They fired me, her father said, and at the time she really didn't com-
prehend the impact of those words that would change her life. Her
teachers at school spoke of recessions and economic crises, but sud-
denly unemployment ceased to be a mere statistic and instead became
a grouchy, unbearable father who now spent the whole day at home.
And at the end of the year she was told that instead of studying, she
would have to get a job.

She takes another look at herself in those new, open high heel shoes
that make her appear taller. The woman who smiles back from the
mirror seems to be somebody else, maybe an actress, or at least one of
those women who struts haughtily in the pages of fashion magazines.
The makeup case always terrifies her. She hears her mother's voice:

43

"Don't paint yourself like a clown." Her mother always worried about good manners. Such a lady. It's getting late. What will Daniel's friends be like? What will they talk about? She dips a piece of cotton in the facial cream and removes the makeup from her eyes only to paint them once again, nervous, trying to make her hand stop shaking, so she doesn't have to start all over again: a thin line, a lot of mascara and that's it. Perfect!

Perfume and anxiousness. She sits on the edge of the bed, looking for her image reflected in the mirror. Where is that woman she sees every day, the one who runs around in blue jeans, laughing with Daniel, provoking him with her ironic barbs—that secretary who prefers to skip lunch to go see the latest exhibition? Here she is hidden beneath the mask of an elegant woman, looking the way her mother looked when things were going well for them, or like her aunts who, whenever they went out, wore leather gloves and very complicated hairdos that could only be controlled with a ton of hair spray. What a shame she'll have to put on that horrible rabbit's fur coat. She hesitates: always before going out she feels that stab of fear, as if she is about to abandon a shelter where she feels protected. Outside, she will no longer be able to undo what's been done, put on something else, excuse herself and not go. And if she doesn't fit in? Will it be awful? Of course not! To be dressed badly isn't such a big deal; there are things that are far more important in this world: misery, war. But that intellectual she so much wanted to be, a secretary, granted, but self-educated through her frequent visits to museums and exhibitions— that woman who says that what matters most are people and not what they're wearing, that same woman knows she is living a lie by spending an inordinate amount of time trying to look elegant, even though she doesn't have much money. But she's afraid to look bad. She couldn't face the embarrassment of knowing that she's somehow inadequate. And when she locked the door with its double lock, she set in motion the irreversible. She takes another look at herself: you really look like a secretary. She decides to leave her overcoat. Rather catch pneumonia. She'll wear the black shawl.

Daniel hadn't given her a clue: a small get-together, a party. He'd shrugged his shoulders to give less importance to the word party. "Just a few friends. I'm sure you'll like them."

"A coming out party," she'd observed in her typically joking tone of voice because that was the personality she'd invented for herself when she arrived in the city, and she enjoyed perfecting this personality for him. She realized that she fascinated him with her playful, challenging answers.

"A happening," replied Daniel, playing along with her.

She takes a final look at herself, like a general reviewing his troops before the attack. Now she really has to get going.

Those months during which she had to make her way through the indifference of the great unknown city and of the imposing company that she worked for. Eight floors, hundreds of employees, and she was just another ant working hard at the ant factory. The architecture department, last floor. "An interesting form," she remarked as she faced the calendar. "Is it a Klee?"

He looked at her, surprised, because architects move in other galaxies, and when she recognized a Klee it showed him she wasn't necessarily an idiot just because she was a secretary. She began to develop a real enthusiasm for those endless jousts of humor and culture in which she would always end up disconcerting him with one of those indifferent replies that only those who have seen and read everything would, perhaps, make. It wasn't true, of course, but she not only represented this type of character, she embodied the type so well that it seemed as if there weren't a single museum she hadn't visited and that her comments—although somewhat sarcastic—weren't completely original.

And that woman of the world she pretended to be, that new persona she invented and perfected every day, that image of the mocking intellectual served as a mask that disguised the little girl from the provinces who tried to get into the university, who cried with emotion the first time she saw a Rembrandt, and who sometimes became desperate at her typewriter, typing up one bureaucratic letter after another while the architects, inclined over their drafting boards, went on designing things completely unaware of the privileges they enjoyed. Now, finally about to enter the world she longed for, just where she should have been from the very beginning, she gives the address to the taxi driver, wondering nervously if she looks good in her black dress. At the same time she hates herself because she knows that her feelings of insecurity are stupid; she shouldn't worry so much. What matters is what they do and say, not what she's wearing.

Laughing, a boy in faded blue jeans and red tennis shoes opens the door and stares at her with a questioning look on his face. Just by the expression in his eyes she realizes she isn't properly dressed. Looking over his shoulder, she sees a part of the room: soft and discreet, a beige wall-to-wall rug; a group chatting on the floor. Not one of the women that she could make out is dressed like she is. One has on a rose-colored velour warm-up suit with matching running shoes, another crosses and uncrosses legs wrapped in leather pants that must have cost more than a month's salary. She sees another one get up slowly and come to the door in frayed blue jeans and a silk smock. She realizes, as if in a sudden revelation, that her shoes are not only out of style but also something only someone from a small town would wear, and it's obvious that her black dress is a Burda design. In those few seconds during which the young woman walks toward her in that disinterested but distinguished way, she tries to overcome the waves of panic that are making her turn red and perspire at the same time. Panic...and rage because they would never let her into a party in her town dressed in those torn blue jeans, and people back home would have said that the woman dressed in the rose-colored warm-up suit was running around in her pajamas and that the other one looked like she just got off a horse.

There wasn't just *one* kind of elegance but many, and she was to blame for interpreting the word party in terms of dresses and jewelry, when as far as Daniel was concerned only middle-class people wore ties and high heels. Why hadn't she figured out that in the happenings he organized, people showed off their casual simplicity and that for them this was elegance. Because good taste is a code that is understood by the in people, and it's always something different and unattainable for the uninitiated. In intense and continuous flashes of insight, she clearly realizes that for them, the big city intellectuals, simplicity is the most sophisticated of styles and she hates herself, for although she considers herself so intelligent and refined, it never occurred to her that her black dress would be ridiculous and gaudy as a neon sign.

Holding the door partly open, the young man, along with the woman dressed in jeans, looks at her. "Who are you looking for," he asks without inviting her in. If he'd spoken to her in the familiar form of address it would have meant that he'd recognized her as belonging to the group, which, of course, is not the case. No one recognizes her; she doesn't see Daniel; she can still say she got off at the wrong floor, take off, run down the stairs, take another taxi, return to her hide-out, lock herself in before he has a chance to see her, before the impact of her *faux pas* becomes irreversible. Tomorrow she could excuse herself with one of her brilliant phrases, she could come up with something: an unexpected visitor, a sick relative. "I didn't have a chance to let you know."

"What a shame; I would have liked you to meet my friends; I spoke so much to them about you."

"You don't know how sorry I am, but you'll invite me again to another happening, won't you?" And the next time she would go dressed in slacks, in boots even, like the women who stay late at the office doing exciting things and who like to be noticed.

"Daniel?" she asks timidly, as if her disguise as an idiot has taken control of her. She feels like fleeing when they have her go in; she imagines locking herself in a bathroom, leaping out the window or covering her face with the black shawl to make sure no one recognizes her. No! I'm not this woman. She's only a poor naive thing who's disguised like me. Beneath the masks and the disguises, where is she? Is she by chance the reserved and distant secretary or the other one, the one who dreams of throwing her typewriter out the window, of pouring paint all over the top of her desk and of painting her passion and fury with her hands. Maybe she's still the girl who wanted to leave her small, stereotypical town, to make time hurry by so she could settle into her own present; the one who broke with the mommy-and-daddy protect me routine and dared to set out on her own. But where was the so-called break if, now that she imagined herself to be free, she kept dressing the way others wanted her to? She, who had always ridiculed the careful-how-you-look, the-make-sure-people-don't-take-you-for-what-you're-not approaches, was now discovering that the contents of her suitcases bore the indelible mark of "what will people say."

In high school, when one of those pretentious girls who tried to look elegant arrived, she and her friends would give her one of those amused looks, a look that slyly took in the poor social climber's outfit, scrutinizing each and every detail, the quality of the material, out-of-style fit, the shoes that didn't match the rest of her outfit, and they would immediately classify her: she's-not-one-of-us. Side glances assessed her lack of upbringing because they already knew that upbringing was important. Accomplices, they winked at each other discreetly: Did you see? Did you notice that...? And with the gestures of great compassionate ladies, even though they were only sixteen years old, they said, "I'm sorry, but I don't think they'll let me go to your house." The cruelty was almost deliberate because at that age you already know with whom to be seen and with whom to associate.

Why had she come dressed in that ridiculous dress, making herself the victim, the stupid social climber, humiliated as she made out just partial gestures, heads that furtively turned with just the requisite slowness so she would realize what was going on. She could almost hear them commenting on her open, high heel shoes and her golden earrings, cataloguing her not for what she was but for what she seemed to be. The arrogant frown of the one in leather pants, and the other in rose, who imperceptibly shrugged her shoulders and turned toward the wall to hide her condescending smile. Alone at the entrance to the room, humiliation invades her completely, deforming her body, which seems to shrink as if disdain can mold and diminish her.

A door opens and Daniel approaches. Tweed trousers, a worn cashmere pull-over and a tray loaded with drinks. "Hi, Daniel" she smiles. His eyes express happiness and puzzlement.

"What did you dress up as?" Did she really hear him say that or did she imagine it? Perhaps it's what that surprised look on his face is asking. She feels like curling up in a corner and howling with rage and frustration.

But no. Not her. Heads or tails. Do it.

"I dressed up as my alter ego," she hears her own voice say decidedly. "I am Woman-object." He observes her, maintaining a certain distance, not showing a single friendly gesture, not saying a single word.

"I am Woman-object," she repeats laughing. "Didn't you tell me it was a happening?"

At last Daniel understands the joke. Echoing her laughter, he carefully places the tray on the carpet, takes her hand and leads her to the center of the room. "I am happy to introduce you to Woman-object," he announces, as if he were the owner of a circus hawking his own show. If looks could kill she would have died the moment they observed her, undecided, still not sure whether to remove this tasteless little idiot from the pigeonhole in which they had placed her.

She can no longer retreat. On the contrary. Get on with it or you're dead. She opens her mouth slightly and flashes a toothpaste commercial smile, then takes several steps forward, giving everyone a big wave as if she were a famous trapeze artist. "Ladies and gentlemen," she says in a loud voice but in the falsetto tone of a clown, "as Woman-object I am happy to initiate for your pleasure tonight's happening."

But nothing happens, nobody laughs. She turns completely around. Nobody reacts. Indifferent eyes produce chills. She takes a deep breath: better eccentric than to have bad taste. She raises her arms and begins to swing her hips, imitating Rita Hayworth as Gilda, and intoning, "Put the blame on Mame, boys," begins to remove one of her leather gloves.

She quickly wonders, "If my aunts, who epitomized the height of elegance in wearing gloves wherever they went, were to see me now, what would they think of this initial strip-tease." A part of her sins as she moves to the rhythm of the song, removing each finger slowly from the glove, taking note (in spite of the fact that her eyes are languidly open) of the interested and even appreciative looks she is getting because it's true that if she dares to imitate the glamorous movie star it is because she's confident not only that she dances well, but that the famous black dress fits her like a glove. But another part of her is terrified by that mad woman now imitating a strip tease, wondering how she's going to get herself out of this mess. In that internal struggle Gilda's imitator, daring and magnificent, prevails over the coward and, tossing the second glove with a theatrical gesture, takes a bow. They applaud her, but she knows it isn't enough; she has to do something else to convince them.

"Ladies and gentlemen," she announces again in the voice of a clown, "in the name of all artists, I have the honor of bestowing on the owner of this circus the surrealistic earring." Removing one of her earrings, she solemnly attaches it to Daniel's pull-over. Hurling the word surrealistic at them immediately after Gilda's dance was like winking at them: she isn't really a Woman-object, she's just acting. And from that moment on she succeeds in making them accomplices; they finally realize that she's one of them, a refined person. Better yet, an eccentric one. And then they applaud her enthusiastically.

But she's so excited she can no longer stop herself. She raises her hands to quiet them. "Ladies and gentlemen, I have a secret to confess." She pauses to intensify the suspense. She slowly removes the other earring and shows it to them as if it were a trophy. This poor little earring that she bought with such illusions; from the jewel that it had been, it is now transformed into an extravagant object. "This precious gem of gold and rubies is the prize that the person who is most bored at the party will win. Any nominations?"

"Pedro!" shouts Daniel.

"No!" protests the woman dressed in the rose-colored warm-up suit, "Juan Pablo's the one. He's the best candidate," she shouts with that big smile that reminds you of a TV announcer. "Gentlemen, begin your nominations." And when everybody starts to take part in the game, she suddenly recognizes Julio Lascasas, the younger generation's best poet (according to the critics), shouting nominations at her for the most bored, and then Toti Langer, the pianist, laughing uncontrollably at Daniel's side. She manages not to feel intimidated in the presence of all those people whose pictures frequently appear in the newspapers. She is too much into the whirlwind of her own game—until she has to stand on tiptoes to pin the earring on a huge man surprised at her kissing him on the cheek. The trump card, she says to herself, because now there are no more looks of compassion. The distance between them and her has been erased; they speak to her, they even fight over getting to know her.

"What's your name, Woman-object," the huge man asks her.

"Cinderella," she replies without hesitating, as if she can think more quickly than they can. "Cinderella," she repeats, "the secretary who went to the ball." And removing one of those horrible shoes of hers, she raises it as high as she can. "I offer my glass slipper to one of the princesses here tonight. A young girl extends a careless finger and she hangs her shoe on it; she takes off the other one and throws it, letting it bounce toward the door. "That's a signal for Prince Charming," she explains calmly.

Suddenly, without her earrings and shoes, she feels a lot better, but she's tired and empty, the way she felt when she returned home after an especially difficult exam. Daniel approachs her with cashews to offer, but this is only a pretext. He really wants to whisper in her ear that his friends find her delightful—that, thanks to her, a real happening is now in full swing because now the Langer woman is playing jazz on a tiny white piano, a discreet little piece of furniture that she hadn't even noticed when she entered the room. Daniel's lips rub against her ear; she feels his warm breath on her neck, and that voice she likes so much it sends chills up and down her spine is now asking her if she's having a good time. Between the emptiness and the euphoria that she's feeling, she allows herself to bask in the pleasure of listening to him, and only then does she forget about the dress she's wearing; she forgets that during the entire day her only concern was with looking elegant, that she spent hours trying to decide whether or not the dress was out of style and whether it matched her colors. Sitting on the beige carpet, she forgets everything so thoroughly and completely that she doesn't even give the slightest thought to that poor, insecure simpleton she had been.

The car's abrupt stop throws her against the back seat. "We're here, Miss," says the taxi driver. "Sorry for stopping like that. I wasn't paying attention. That's the building you want."

Translated by John J. Hassett.
From Volume 9: *What Is Secret*

MARTA JARA

THE ENGLISHWOMAN

I saw her arrive one night at nine o'clock, gaunt, pale, blonde and at that indefinite age of some Englishwomen, somewhere between twenty-five and sixty years old. In her hand she carried an old suitcase and, resting on her recently permed curls, an unstylish hat, yellowed and faded.

"Miss Hutchinson...I'm Miss Emily Hutchinson...," she stammered in English with an awkward, pathetic voice, when, after the apprehensive sound of the bell, we rushed to the front door. She gave my parents a vigorous handshake and, looking at me kindly, asked me my name. I remained silent.

"Answer," ordered my father, severely. "It's the English governess who has come from Europe."

"I will never answer her," I responded timidly, "I don't like her..."

My parents looked at each other, horrified. Looking back, I think my father's eyes said, "I have made a great financial sacrifice. The governess has come on a freighter, cheap to be sure but still too expensive for my earnings. A great sacrifice. And this stubborn little girl..."

"She's very tired," explained my mother. "Tomorrow's another day."

Days, months, a year passed. And I continued to act haughty in my rebelliousness. "Doesn't she understand, it's for her own good?" my father would exclaim. "Doesn't she see the benefits I'm trying to give her? Doesn't she feel it's necessary, indispensable, to know English? Having another language is like having another soul." And seeing my lowered head and sullen expression, he would grasp his head with both hands murmuring, "Some children are such donkeys! Donkeys!" Meanwhile, I envied the luck of my brother, who, after school and with our two cousins, took lessons with Mr. Bingle, an exuberant Englishman, light-hearted and eccentric, who quickly became my teacher too.

"Fine," warned my father one day, looking at me resolutely. "As long as you keep acting this way, you won't get any dessert."

"If you want, I'll answer 'yes,' but no more than 'yes,' " I agreed, letting out one of those deep breaths children take before crying.

That "yes" was the only connection between my small self and the Englishwoman who, each day in the house, felt more alone and more disoriented, enduring the tremendous loneliness of exile, to which was added the isolation of not being able to speak or understand. She knew no Spanish and no one in the family spoke English. A terrible form of prison. Until one day, seeing the uselessness of her presence in our home, my father sent her back to her country.

Poor Emily Hutchinson. Today, when I think of you, something quivers and stirs in the bottom of my heart. One day you embarked on a trip, very far away, prompted by the urgency of your unknown destiny, leaving behind the few belongings and humble memories that until then had made your life bearable. The embroidery in the pattern of a cross, and your needle, remained unfinished in the old drawer of the bureau. And the clumsy table clock, inherited from your grandmother, solitarily chimed the hours in the boarding house. You left for hostile climates and surroundings and your story became entwined with that of all the unfortunate and anonymous souls whose insignificance drags along, moribund and hidden. Souls who never realize their great ambition. And—as you know, Emily Hutchinson—between toiling and uprooting, life passes, slowly withering away like a tree that hasn't been watered.

Children cause suffering without realizing it. Later, through a magnifying glass, they look at the harm they unknowingly caused. And they would give the world to change it. But they can't always touch the ashes of the past.

Today, I don't know why, from the depths of my childhood I see the aimless Englishwoman arrive with her absurd hat and her gaunt figure. An immense pity, a longing to pronounce the word that my childish lips didn't know how to say, wells up with the quickening beats of my heart.

Translated by Jennifer Bayon and Doris Meyer.
From Volume 9: *What Is Secret*

LAURA RIESCO

AN EXCERPT FROM
XIMENA AT THE CROSSROADS

The next evening, at Aunt Alejandra's request, Ximena and her mother hunt for the old family photographs, the ones they always intend to put in an album but which continue to pile up in two cigar boxes and a big manila envelope. Ximena stays right with them, even though her father has offered to play checkers with her. She has hardly ever had a chance to see these photos because her mother feels guilty about their being in such disorder and prefers to not even think about the dark corner of her closet where they have been for years. Her aunt especially wants to see the pictures of Crazy Grandmother because she is writing some short pieces about her.

"I don't know why my mother kept so few of these. I want to see all the ones you have, from the time she was little until the very last pictures."

Her hands search through the pile of various-sized photos, some already frayed and others which have held up better over the years because they are as thick as postcards or were artistically framed in cardboard by the studio. Her aunt's long, slim fingers make her think of her mother's, but her aunt's are stronger and more agile, and Ximena, staring at them, imagines that they are like the outstretched wings of roosters at dawn. Gretchen looks at the backs of the photos. "But there are no names or dates here. How will you be able to recognize her as a child or as a young woman?"

"I'll recognize her by the look on her face. When you come across one with a rebellious expression, looking as though she is yelling a decisive 'No!' to the whole world, that is our grandmother."

Ximena wishes they would look at all the photos one by one, even if they were not of the grandmother. She would like to see all the other relatives, too: ladies with parasols, with very narrow waists and heart-shaped bustles; boys who look just like their sisters because they have the same haircuts and because they are all wearing baggy blouses or sailor suits; several of a naked baby sleeping face down on a big shiny, dark cushion; men dressed up in their Sunday suits, with sideburns that connect with their beards, mustaches with pointy tips, their jackets unbuttoned in a gesture which is clearly meant to show off the gold watches hanging from their vest pockets. Sometimes Aunt Alejandra makes them laugh by imitating the exaggeratedly erect posture and the patriarchal seriousness of these relatives. "Just look at this couple! As though they had gotten dressed and had forgotten to remove the coat hangers!"

But she does not linger long on these. She hunts for the ones she wants and puts them to one side. Crazy Grandmother, whom Ximena remembers only as a shadow by the window of the room where they had her locked up at the house in the valley, is easy to identify because she does not pose like the other girls and young women. Even in pictures of her when she is younger than Ximena is now, there is something defiant and mocking in the way she stares.

"She was a real character, an exceptional woman," sighs her aunt. "Imagine the stories she could tell us if she were alive!"

"She was totally out of her mind," replies her mother. "Why do you think they had to lock her up first in Lima and then on the *hacienda?*"

"They locked her up because she wouldn't let herself be tamed, because from very early on, she threw away all regard for proper manners and the family reputation in provincial society, in order to live as she pleased."

Ximena observes her mother's increasing tension. The skin around her mouth is stiffening the way it does when they contradict her and she gets mad. "You may see her as a literary character, but she was a woman of flesh and blood and caused the family lots of problems with her bizarre behavior and her temperament. They should have taught her a lesson early on and put her behind bars. All it got her was that they excluded her more and more often and when they did invite her to social events, it was only because of her family name or because they knew she would play the eccentric clown and liven up dances. They laughed at her. And you know full well," she adds, speaking in a louder and louder voice, faster and faster, to Ximena's dismay, "that she never settled down, and she was a bad wife and a worse mother. If she had any excuse, it was that she suffered from her nerves, and there were all those entire days when she would close herself up and not see anyone. Remember how we used to spy on her during those strange spells when she filled her room with incense and, wrapped in a sheet, prayed to Hindu gods as though she didn't have a religion of her own? And why so much mysticism? It just put everyone off. If people felt sorry for her, it was because she was out of her mind."

Ama Grande, as though she were connected by threads of premonition, without anyone having called her, comes in early from the kitchen to put Ximena to bed. While she tries to escape, without anyone noticing, from the big rough hands that, in a gesture her body knows all too well, are trying to push her toward the bathtub, Gretchen stares at her openly and Ximena feels ashamed. She would have liked to protest and plead to stay up for at least a few more minutes, but she feels found out and exposed, and she snuggles up against the comforting embrace of Ama Grande's layers of skirts, until she almost disappears in the sheltering folds.

Translated by Mary G. Berg.
From Volume 12: *Ximena at the Crossroads*

ALFONSINA STORNI

MEN IN THE CITY

The forests of the
horizon burn;
dodging flames,
the blue bucks
of the twilight
cross quickly.

Little gold goats
emigrate toward
the arch of the sky
and lie down
on blue moss.

Below,
there rises,
enormous,
the cement rose,
the city
unmoving on its stem
of somber basements.

Its black pistils—
dormers, towers—
emerge
to wait for lunar
pollen.

Suffocated
by the flames of bonfires,
and lost
among the petals

of the rose,
almost invisible,
moving from one side toward the other,
the men...

NIGHT

Thanks, night:
not because the moon returns
or the stars lie
or the crickets sing
in the damp marble.

Thanks because you dissolve
the dirtiness of the streets
with your invisible veils.

Translated by Marion Freeman.

LITANY FOR A DEAD EARTH

For Gabriela Mistral

There will come a day when the human race
Will have dried up like a dead vine,

And the ancient sun will be
Like the useless ashes of a burned torch.

There will come a day on the frozen earth
When there will be a sad and total silence:

A huge shadow will encircle the earth
And spring will never return;

The dead earth, like a blind eye,
Will go on turning without peace forever

But in the darkness, all alone, groping
Without a song or a moan or a prayer.

All alone, with her favorite creatures
Exhausted and sleeping in her womb.

(Like a mother who goes on even though she has
The poison of dead children in her womb.)

No city will be standing...the earth will support
Ruins and rubbish on her dead shoulders.

From a distance black mountains
Will look on without caring.

Maybe the sea will be nothing more
Than a block of ice, dark like all the rest.

And then, anguished and motionless,
It will dream of ships and waves,

And pass the years trying to ambush
Any boat that plows through its breast,

Where the sea meets the earth
It will create illusions on the beach with the moon,

It will try to make
the moon another mausoleum.

Uselessly the block of ice will want to open its mouths
To swallow rocks and men,

To hear the horrible screams
Of shipwrecked sailors wailing endlessly:

Nothing will remain; from pole to pole
A single wind will have wept it all away:

The seductive palaces of Spain
And the miserable huts of Bedouins;

The hidden caves of Eskimos
And lavish delicate cathedrals.

Blacks, yellows, browns,
Whites, malays, mestizos...

They wil meet beneath the earth
Begging each other's pardon for so much war.

Holding hands they will surround
The entire earth in a circle.

Perhaps some gentle star
Will ask: "Who is she?

Who is this statue of a woman who dares
To move by herself through a dead world?"

And it will love her by celestial instinct
Until she falls at last from her pedestal.

Perhaps one day, because of some nameless mercy,
The light of a wandering sun

Will rekindle in its fire
This poor earth and its people.

And will timidly suggest to it: O tired earth
Dream for a moment of spring!

Absorb me for an instant: I am
The universal soul which changes and never rests...

How they will move beneath the earth,
Those dead who are closed inside her womb!

How they will push toward divine light
Wanting to fly toward what enlightens them!

Those dead eyes will try in vain
To reach the red rays.

In vain! In vain! The mud piled
Over their bones will be too thick...

Defeated and stacked together
They will not be able to leave their ancient nests,

And to the call of a passing star
No one will be able to cry: I love!

Translated by Jim Normington.
From Volume 1: *Alfonsina Storni: Selected Poems*

Anabel Torres

A Small Miracle

If only a small miracle
occurred,
if the cook
slipped out of her horrible uniform
like a tired
trickle
leaking from the faucet,

and on the pavement
at midnight
a taxi were waiting for her.

Translated by Celeste Kostopulos-Cooperman.
From Volume 7: *These Are Not Sweet Girls*

GABRIELA MISTRAL

THE LARK

You said that you loved the lark more than any other bird because of its straight flight toward the sun. That is how I wanted our flight to be.

Albatrosses fly over the sea, intoxicated by salt and iodine. They are like unfettered waves playing in the air, but they do not lose touch with the other waves.

Storks make long journeys; they cast shadows over the earth's face. But like albatrosses, they fly horizontally, resting in the hills.

Only the lark leaps out of ruts like a live dart and rises, swallowed by the heavens. Then the sky feels as though the earth itself has risen. Heavy jungles below do not answer the lark. Mountains crucified over the flatlands do not answer.

But a winged arrow quickly shoots ahead, and it sings between the sun and the earth. One does not know if the bird has come down from the sun or risen from the earth. It exists between the two, like a flame. When it has serenaded the skies with its abundance, the exhausted lark lands in the wheat field.

You, Francis, wanted us to achieve that vertical flight, without a zigzag, in order to arrive at that haven where we could rest in the light.

You wanted the morning air filled with arrows, with a multitude of carefree larks. Francis, with each morning song, you imagined that a net of golden larks floated between the earth and the sky.

We are burdened, Francis. We cherish our lukewarm rut: our habits. We exalt ourselves in glory, just as the towering grass aspires. The loftiest blade does not reach beyond the high pines.

Only when we die do we achieve that vertical flight. Never again, held back by earthy ruts, will our bodies inhibit our souls.

Translated by Maria Giachetti.
From Volume 5: *A Gabriela Mistral Reader*

Sara Gallardo

The Man in the Araucaria

A man spent twenty years making himself a pair of wings. In 1924, he tried them out at dawn. They worked with a slow swinging motion. They didn't take him any higher than thirty-six feet, as high as an araucaria in the Plaza of San Martín.

The man abandoned his wife and children to spend more hours in the top of the tree. He worked for an insurance company. He moved into a boarding house. Each night at midnight, he put sewing machine oil on his wings and walked off to the plaza. He carried them in a violincello case.

He had a nest at the top of the tree, comfortable enough. It even had pillows.

At night, life in the plaza is extraordinarily complex, but he never bothered to get into it. The foliage, the dark houses, and especially the stars, were enough for him. The nights when the moon was out were the best.

Our problem is not accepting limits. He got it in his head to spend a whole day in his nest. It was a company holiday.

The sun came up. There's nothing like dawn in the treetops.

Very high up, a flock of birds passed, leaving the city at their feet. He contemplated them with a kind of dizziness, with tears.

That was what he had dreamed about during the twenty years he had dedicated to constructing his wings. Not about an araucaria.

He blessed the birds. He lost his heart to them.

A maid opened the shutters in the house of an aged, sleepless woman. She saw the man in his nest. The old lady called the police and the fire department.

With loudspeakers, with ladders, they surrounded him.

It took him some time to see what was happening. He put on his wings. He stood up.

The cars put on their brakes. People gathered. Windows opened. He saw his children with their school smocks. His wife with her shopping bag. The maids and the old ladies holding on to each other.

The wings worked, slowly. He touched branches.

But he lost altitude. He went down as far as the monument. He leapt. He got entangled in the horse's haunches. He grabbed San Martín by the waist. He was smiling.

He got as far as the English tower; the wind helped him along toward the south.

He lives between the smoke pipes of a factory. He is old and eats chocolate.

Translated by Elizabeth Rhodes.
From Volume 4: *Secret Weavers.*

DORA ALONSO

CAGE NUMBER ONE

The monkey's eyes shone in the dawn light, peering in every direction. Getting up, she crept toward the bars of the cage, overcome by the desire to escape confinement. Her belly was full and she wasn't troubled by lust, but she needed contact with the leaves that had surrounded her since she first opened her wrinkled eyelids in that place.

Every night, as she crouched in her cement cubicle at the back of the cage, the last thing she saw were the trees. When she awoke, she looked for them. If there was wind, or if it rained, the rain polished them; if the tiny leaves danced and the thunder made the buds tremble, the monkey watched, feeling herself fill up with green shoots that were born of her longing—ungraspable, tenacious...

She watched vaguely, motionless under the swaying branches that swept above the cage. Her mother, her grandmother, twenty generations of primates contemplated the leaves through her fixed gaze.

With her snout encased in a funnel of black, flexible and lukewarm skin, she held fast to the bars. Above her, the whispering of the seeds telling secrets began, the tide of rising sap in the shadow, the single words from the branches broken by the heavy dew... She stood still, her thin hand suspended in the air, not feeling the need to mortify her flesh with the hunter's thumb anymore. Uneasiness sharpened her teeth, pressed on her temples. She screeched in fright and curled herself up with her arms behind her head to protect herself from some fear that lurked nearby, the moist dawn grass.

Terror made her crouch next to the concrete, an eternal wall. The same words, the same voice, the song, the lisp, spoke to her always, calling her. Every muscle in her body wanted to respond at once. She jumped, but as she did she whimpered indecisively. She babbled on, shaken by a restlessness that was killing her.

Approaching the bars for a second time, she held on with both hands and showed her black face, long and sorrowful as a death mask. The iron felt cold and hostile. Its smoothness penetrated the tips of her fingers and she encircled the bars with her whole hand, squeezing hard. Surging with fury, she shook the bars. The iron began to yield and bend. The monkey walked through.

Now that she was calmer, the snores from Pipa's cubs and the trailing of a lizard through the dry brush did not disturb her.

From his circular cage, the gibbon cried, hanging his lament from the expectant trees on long-faded branches.

The monkey passed like a shadow through the stillness of the sleeping park.

The great prison breathed in the night, liberating its vegetable dreams, the tortured nightmares of free rivers and rapid deaths, the fever of sterile encounters, the castrated anger of confinement.

She trotted aimlessly, touching the earth with the knuckles of her closed hands, her head low. What was born that night kept shaking her with the cooing of the wind, with the breath, the complaint, the secret.

She stopped at the tree: it was weeping leaves and sighs. The monkey's eyes filled up like two wells of happiness. The mantle spilled over, pouring silk and freshness from above. Everything scorching her inside was extinguished. Oh, oh, oh, the chatter of monkeys drenched her with happiness. Oh, oh. She climbed up the trunk and its roughness penetrated her, bleeding her of unknown flowers. Embracing the tree, she tried to grasp it and drink what was coursing beneath the bark.

She touched a branch with her forehead and the wet leaves brushed lips that were desperately pressed together. She moaned and moaned, closing her eyes, languid with fever. The bowls of water and fruit, the swing and the hoop were very far away on this first free morning.

The monkey was delirious, dreaming she was biting the good keeper on the throat until she could feel her lips near his flowing arteries; she strangled him with the shoelaces that he had taught her to tie and untie. She dreamed she was fleeing to the forest, followed by all the simians deformed in exhibitions:

Orangutans from the dense jungles of Sumatra and Borneo, red like living flames, the "savage men" of the far-off island.

Gibbons from the islands of Indonesia, the beloved Unka-Pati of Malaysia with long arms, agile as arrows.

Patriarchal gorillas from the plains and from the mountains, skilled at climbing and hanging from branches; like sailors, masters of a hundred knots. Two hundred kilos of defeated bulk and several meters wide when they stretched out their arms.

Chimpanzees of inconceivable force, impetuous, of the highest intelligence; white-faced, black-faced, bald, pygmies, flying through the branches when they heard the tom-tom of the leader of the herd on the hollow trunks, ordering the beginning of the war dance.

The monkey felt them close behind her, in an unending multitude...

Baboons with gaudy reddish callouses; short-tailed, omnivorous mandrills, their beastly bluish masks striped with colors, the untiring trot. Papions sacred to India, warlike, shrewd, stone-throwers. Their rival baboons. Amadrias with thick shoulder capes, worshipped by the ancient Egyptians.

Grotesque rhinotipecs with brilliant blue skin and large turned up noses, from the eternal snows of Tibet; petty thieves, crazed by the flasks...

Angry green monkeys.

Frantic macaques, swimmers and collectors of algae and crabs, native to Japan, the Philippines, China, Java, with long tails and pink faces.

There were a thousand noises: wails, trills, chirps, barks, whistles, grunts.

They descended in waves from the Old World, joining monkeys of America with prehensile tails. From the Sierra Madre to Paraguay, the members of the great desolate family came from the young continent.

Beautiful black and copper-colored howlers, inhabitants of the torrential jungles of the Amazon basin.

Capuchins, curious and blinking like little old people.

Spider monkeys, like mute dummies.

Pacific fat-bellies.

Micos from Peru, from Matto Grosso, eaters of grasshoppers and scorpions.

Multicolored herds of silky titis: titi-lion cub, its mane of fluff virgin gold, golden yellow: white feathery titis from barren Catinga; squirrel titis and ones with paintbrush hair...

Coveted pygmy monkeys from Ecuador, weighing eighty grams

(jewel and ambition of courtesans), with newborn hands that a magnifying glass can barely uncover.

The colored dwarves came leaping over the vast green heights. Their long caravan was joined by the monkeys enslaved in circuses and by street musicians.

The diseased, blind monkeys ran stumbling, saved from the distant aristocratic properties of Havana, when their forgetful owners, fleeing from the armed populace, left the country, condemning them to death by starvation.

There came others, degenerated by captivity: those who had destroyed each other with their teeth in the rampant fire, finding no escape for their inhibited desire. The sadistic and murderous Martín Pérez. And the pleasure-hungry cripple forced by the law of demand to satisfy himself with any living thing that moved nearby: pigeon, man, tiger or frog.

At the front line, with tooth and nail, the great Toto, the trusty chimpanzee who threw excrement, spat at the curious, at children, old people, soldiers or women whom he attacked with his imprisoned sex.

The delirious fugitive penetrated the fragrant green foliage curtain, possessing it for all those of her species who suffered imprisonment, with her nerves, her brain and her eyes covered and laced with roots, leaves and invisible, untouched branches.

The hairy hands with the opposing thumb grasped the branches. They broke one, hanging it at the crown of the tree to start a nest. As she snapped the branch in two and wove it into place, the sun came out.

* * *

Along the avenue where the flamboyán trees opened their red umbrellas, a keeper was arriving. He stopped in front of cage number one, looked inside and shouted to send the word to the dwarf: "Look, Simon: the monkey's dead!"

Translated by Miriam Ben-Ur and Lorraine Elena Roses.
From Volume 3: Landscapes of a New Land

AMALIA RENDIC

A BOY, A DOG, THE NIGHT

The sun faded shortly in golden rays. The faint light of the street-lamps could scarcely hold back the darkness and fog that invaded the entire mining camp. A large group of men handling the pile drivers, machinists, ore workers, and miners were going home. The return journey was slow and silent because of the thin air caused them to breathe with difficulty. The Chuquicamata mine is situated at over two thousand eight hundred meters above sea level.

As the group arrived at the Binkeroft neighborhood, it began to disperse toward the workers' camp. Household lights could be seen through half-open windows and doors. The worker, Juan Labra, a strong machinist and loyal friend, continued walking on one of the many narrow streets, still sighing because of the shrill whistles and sirens of the work areas. The wrinkles quickly vanished from his young face, which was already furrowed with deep lines like veins of ore, and a burst of tenderness filled his eyes. He readily accepted his young family's loving welcome. Little Juan was waiting at the door of the house as he did every afternoon. He was a small nine-year-old boy, with lively curious eyes, quite strong for his age, and with feet that loved to walk. For him, the mine had no secrets. He knew every inch of the mine and all of its mysteries. He was a talkative child whose constant chatter could be interrupted only by smiles. With his face pressed against the iron garden gate, he curiously watched a very tall North American who was walking behind his father.

"Dad, a *gringo* is following you, he is coming to our house!" he whispered, frightened, to his father. The street was deserted. Little Juan was intrigued by the presence of Black, the huge shepherd dog that followed Mr. Davies, his master. Black was one of the few beings that had managed to gain Davies' affections. A solitary companion in his lonely existence in a foreign land.

"Please come in, Mr. Davies. What can we do for you?"asked the miner, Juan Labra, respectfully taking off his metal hat and opening the small door of the gate. He could barely hide his astonishment at seeing one of the company's owners at his door.

"I'll be brief, Mr. Labra. I need a big favor from you. I soon must leave for Antofagasta and want to leave in your custody for a few days my good friend, Black. You'll be kind. In Calama you organized a society for the protection of animals. Everybody knows this," said Mr. Davies, looking at his dog.

"That's fine, Mr. Davies. Thank you for your trust. He will be happy here. We will make sure the dog doesn't suffer. My son, Little Juan, will take care of him in my absence," promised Labra, adjusting his jacket and feeling strangely satisfied inside.

"I leave him in your hands and thank you very much. See you later, Mr. Labra. I'll return very soon, Black...Ah, I forgot! Here, I'll leave his provisions of canned meat. It is his favorite food."

The master and his dog seemed sad. Black tugged at his master's pants; Davies bent over to pet the dog's head, with its pointed snout, and left. The animal started to follow, but Little Juan's arms held him back like chains. Black barked falteringly, sniffing the air. His red, wet tongue was hanging out of his mouth. He panted anxiously. The boy closed the gate. Black stood erect, looking lonesome. His shining fur, his slenderness, his dignified bearing were indications of his pedigree. He was an expensive dog and had won many dog shows because of his pedigree.

The boy began talking to the dog as if it were a younger brother. For a long time they watched each other without even blinking. The dog's gaze was steady, and the boy's face was reflected in his eyes like tiny bright points. He shyly petted the back of the dog, who was sniffing the air and later responded with a reluctant movement of his tail.

Little Juan continued his strange monologue with Black. They started to become fond of each other. Across the dark, foggy hours of the night the dawn arrived. Then the day broke as always, in the middle of the two huge mounds that formed the San Pedro and San Pablo volcanoes. Everything seemed to be a wet blue color.

Black awoke with the first sirens on the patio of the worker's house and watched the procession of miners; it was almost as if a great thing had awakened in his heart, too. He responded to these new impressions with barks that sounded like explosions. First thing in the morning, Little Juan, in a fantasy world, went out to see his new friend, and during the next few days they went everywhere together.

Challenging the wind, they ran along the winding ribbon that was the road to Calama. They tirelessly penetrated the immense vastness of the thin air.

They played together, diving into the grey residues of the copper mine pit, that shapeless, majestic mass of metallic land. They tried to collect the shining blue-green and yellow reflections that make bright colors in the sunlight.

They passed the hours this way until the nights came, the ties of the friendship that bound Little Juan and Black becoming stronger and stronger. A growing anxiety clouded the boy's short-lived happiness. He was dreading the day that their time together would end. It was certain that Mr. Davies would return.

"Papa, can't you ask the mister to give us Black? Why can't you buy him?"

"No, Little Juan, he will never be ours. He is very elegant and worth his weight in gold. He is a rich man's dog. The *gringos* like to take walks with dogs like this one and present them in shows," answered the worker with a bitter smile.

"When I grow up I will buy him," responded little Juan decisively. "I don't want them to take him away! He's my friend!" he shouted at his father.

One day, as they returned from their walk on the banks of the Loa River, a nasty mountain wind began to blow. They were wet from the silky mist of Camanchaca. When they came to the door, they stopped as if in fear and dread.

"Mr. Davies!" He had returned. The little boy tried to explain what the dog meant to him, but the words welled up in his heart and stayed in his parched throat. It was a sad moment.

"Goodbye, little friend, and good luck," he stammered, weeping and wringing his hands nervously.

Mr. Davies thanked him sincerely. Like a little gentleman, the child refused to accept any payment.

Black reluctantly started to walk behind his former owner and, eagerly examining the corners of the road, said goodbye to the workers' neighborhoods on the road toward the American camp. Now that

Little Juan's first encounter with despair was over, he pondered the fact that he could never have an elegant dog. Black continued his walk. The harmony settled in both of them.

But the loneliness of night came, when souls contemplate themselves to the last fragment of life itself, and then everything was useless. Little Juan's defenses collapsed, and he began to cry. Something provoked a flow of communication between the boy and the animal across the space, and at that very moment, the dog began to howl in the American camp. Memories of Black were flashing through the boy's mind and, as if driven by a secret force, the dog barked furiously, asking the wind to transmit his message. It began as a plaintive concert, and then it became deafening.

Little Juan cried the whole night in a beseeching moan that became a strange concert that whipped through the still streets of the mining town.

Mr. Davies was bewildered by Black's behavior. What could a man do when faced with a crying dog? A new truth took possession of the *gringo's* mind. Black didn't belong to him anymore; he had lost his love.

Labra could not comfort his tearful and feverish little boy. For what could a man do when faced with a crying child? Labra wanted to see his son's quick, confident smile once again. He felt obliged to win back Little Juan's smile. Poverty had stung him many times, but he could not stand this. Something extraordinary would have to happen in the mining town on this uneasy night.

As if the time had come for all men to be brothers, Labra threw his poncho on his shoulders, took the flashlight, and set off for the high neighborhood to see if a miracle could become reality. Yes, he must be courageous and daring. He, a simple laborer, always shy and silent, would ask for the elegant, beautiful, prize-winning Black from one of the company bosses. He inhaled the cold night air deeply and shuddered to think of his own boldness. He climbed up toward the American camp.

Suddenly, a pair of brown, phosphorescent eyes were glowing in the light of the lantern. Labra was startled. The smell of a pipe and fine tobacco and a familiar bark stopped him...

Mr. Davies had gone out to see him at that very moment and had been coming toward the workers' housing area! Something touched the hearts of the two men. Words were not necessary.

"He doesn't belong to me anymore," stammered Mr. Davies, depositing Black's heavy metal leash in the worker's hands.

Labra took the animal in his trembling hands and a melancholy happiness warmed his smile. There were no elaborate thanks, only a silent and reciprocal understanding. Black, tugging, forced him to continue following his tracks toward Little Juan's neighborhood. In that miraculous moment, a new warmth tempered the night of Chuqui.

Translated by Miriam Ben-Ur.
From Volume 3: *Landscapes of a New Land*

Rosario Ferré

You Have Lost, They Tell Me, Your Reason

you have lost, they tell me, your reason
hear me well

when you go down the street
everyone points a finger at your cocked head
as if they wanted to blow it off you
only pull the trigger and boom!
your forehead caves in on you like a beer can

don't say hello to anyone
don't comb your hair, don't shine your shoes
cross the street on your own arm
take your own hand, button your collar
stay alert

there goes the crazy man, they say

you go bobbing by your dusty head
like a wooden saint taken out for a parade
your feet nailed to the worm-eaten platform
looking in the distance
don't let your flesh ripen
let yourself be stoned

you have lost, it is evident, your reason
listen well
tie yourself tightly to the mast
bind yourself to the polar star
don't unhinge the ancient planks now
don't raise the oars from their pivots

fix your sharpest eye on the star
remain constant
don't blink but from time to time
sleep tranquilly on your fists
don't be afraid to remember
close your glass-cutting teeth
cage your tongue
don't swallow anymore
you have lost your reason, friend, now it's time
cut the cord
climb up to the wind
harden your heart

Translated by Nancy Díaz.
From Volume 7: *These Are Not Sweet Girls*

SECTION II
WOMEN AND GENDER

ANABEL TORRES

THESE ARE THE SWEET GIRLS

These are
the sweet girls
who go to the matinée.
These are
the sweet girls
prepared to be the echo,
prepared to be the small round pebble in the center
stirring the concentric
circles
while the waves move further and further away.

These are
the girls with smooth
skin
and a soul
even smoother and,
without curves.

Translated by Celeste Kostopulos-Cooperman.
From Volume 7: *These Are Not Sweet Girls*

MAGALI GARCÍA RAMOS

AN EXCERPT FROM

HAPPY DAYS, UNCLE SERGIO

We always asked "why." Sometimes we had the impression that adults left thoughts unfinished precisely to get us to ask why, so that they could make speeches. That was how they tried to indoctrinate us with a mixture of scientific and religious concepts, true and false, liberal and conservative, products of their fears and prejudices, their wisdom and beliefs; information which took us a lifetime to reorganize and debunk.

It was implicit in Life itself that there was Good and Evil and whether it was admitted openly or in passing, we knew that every action, every individual and every idea was judged by our family according to this standard of Good and Evil.

On the good side were the Catholic, Apostolic and Roman Religion, the Pope, the United States, the Americans, Eisenhower, Europe, especially all the refined Europeans, Grace Kelly, white people, all the militaries, Franco, Evita Perón, opera, *zarzuelas*, everything Spanish, including *mantillas*, sausages and the singer, Sarita Montiel, and absolutely everything German and Swiss, from Rhine wines to cuckoo clocks.

On the evil side were the communists, atheists, Protestants, nazis, newly formed black African nations (because in the process they spilled European blood and killed nuns), Puerto Rican nationalists and any Puerto Ricans in favor of independence, mambo, Trujillo, Batista, and the Mexican actress, María Felix, the wicked woman responsible for Jorge Negrete being in hell.

"When he was about to die," explained Sara F., as if she had been there, "the priest came to him and said: 'Do you abjure that woman?' and he answered no, so he didn't receive absolution and he went straight to hell when he died, because he had lived with her out of wedlock." That's why we could not see her movies, not even on television;

80

it was unforgivable to be a bad woman. "Do you go to hell if you live with someone who is not your husband?" These were the clues about being an adult that intrigued us.

"No, not if you live in the same house, like in a guest house or a hotel, only if you live together, like when Mamá puts the doves in a cage together."

"But she marries them," we answered. When Mamá Sara caught a pair of doves and put them together in a small cage or a box she always said, "I'm marrying them." She was like a priestess; she had that power. Priests were the only ones with that power on land and sea captains at sea, but in our yard Mamá Sara had that authority.

"Well anyway, it's the fault of the woman," concluded Sara F. "Women who misbehave are evil, they do it out of viciousness. On the other hand, men often can't avoid it. Men have a wolf inside..."

Translated by Carmen C. Esteves.
From Volume 8: *Happy Days, Uncle Sergio*

Marta Blanco

Maternity

It's positive they told me and that's that, not a thing to be done about it, what happiness, can you imagine your whole life changing just like that, swelling up with maternal pride at this huge surprise, maybe it's even twins I thought, and what a beautiful day it was, blue and transparent—one of those days you got so used to up here at the house in the mountains, when the snow would seem about to slide right through the dining room window and the kids took early showers and drained the hot water heater with their sporadic bursts of hygienic zeal, and the coffee smells wonderful, fresh and rich, and it's barely seven o'clock in the morning and it's time to comb the youngest one's hair, she has hair like a porcupine poor thing, but she's so lovely; I hadn't the slightest doubt about it being good news, in addition to giving me back a sense of my own maternal identity that goes along with being a young woman, right, and no one likes to walk around feeling incomplete, it's a little like having just one eye, and you had always wanted a child, once you'd even wept, you were really good at weeping, because the two of us weren't able to have a child and all because it was my fault, sterile I assumed, stupid fool, and maybe that's why I looked after and cared so much about yours, who dated from before, from way back, from your previous life and that's not so unheard of, what with the problem of annulments this country gobbles up the poor women who are dragging babies around with them, there's not a thing to do about it if the other person won't sign the paper, so you end up living alone on pure love and who was going to doubt that, not me, I was all wrapped up in cotton candy, I was a candied chestnut, sweet as syrup and always being careful of your pride, which is a bigger deal than protecting the Pope's pride, boy do I know your weak spots, that's why I never asked you for anything that was off limits, never talked about what's prohibited or impossible, marriage didn't enter into our secret language, we were together out of need for love, in daily busyness and friendliness, in a mysterious state of grace, a modern alliance, and I listened to Pedro Vargas every day because that was part of the repertory of your personal obsessions even though sometimes I'd have liked Watusi or "When I left Cuba" and sometimes at sunset I yearned for Vivaldi, all that when I was tuned in to culture, but you always preferred Bach, and the sonatas made my heart ache, they were too violent, I wanted to regard them as incomprehensible, what else could you do with those sonatas that announce death I said and that's how it turned out, how could I have known I had an aptitude as a Cassandra, fortunetellers amused me, although sometimes I sought them out, like that time with the witch on Mariposa Hill, in Valparaiso, who smoked a cigar and read the cards and turned out to be a shitty witch because the truth was something altogether different, totally different, and now I'm caught up in this melancholy that makes me feel curiously languid, but it must be the sun, which makes me dizzy with its heat, and the house, which is still full of familiar sounds and furniture that is too solid, it should be ghost-like, vaporize at the slightest hint that the established order is perturbed, it's very hard to stay on in the same place, send down roots, love the places where one is most oneself in some way: I always envied you that, your great capacity for flight, for change, for sleep, that incredible ability to keep moving along without looking back was dangerous, no one is happy and the next minute miserable, no one should have that capacity for flight and be that close to people, love them furiously, chase after them, write them letters, become part of their lives and then like someone who isn't even doing it on purpose, just all of a sudden walk right out the door one day because that's it and how can we help it and you're reborn just like that, you submerge yourself in the baptismal font, and shazam you're a new man and you go right back to the game of adoring—and adorning—and the next poor girl falls for it because it's so hard to resist the words which transform the world into a game of mirrors, the stained glass is so gorgeous, we saw Saint Chapelle together, do you remember, and it was like being beyond this world, transported by all the light the glass transfigured and because the play of the sun through the blue and that deep red is truly disorienting, hallucinogenic, so that now I had the security and had passed the test and all that I said okay now, this puts me into a new position, into a pretty good position at the least and human beings should love each other, isn't that what the commandments say, what a bastardly thing to abandon a pregnant woman, the whole scene was just too romantic, I was eating myself up with love for you and it seemed as though you were about to love me a little, give me back just a little bit of what I'd given you in so many years of living together and supporting each other, and that even though one does these things without knowing why, there are moments in life when you just have to risk it all for someone, go for broke, especially since you were so alone and abandoned, so wretched and miserable when you fell into my arms, I'd have sworn that you loved me, it's revolting to feel that I was your feather pillow, with the soul of a feather comforter the poor dear, barely a rung on your career ladder of liberation and aspiration, but I'd have sworn that right now you were going to react decently, I'd have sworn it, couldn't you just die laughing, how could I possibly have guessed that you couldn't stand me, it was absurd, there was no clue, no hint of that at all, except that you raced out and said you had to think it over, whatever happened you had to think it over, an equation is something you believe is set in concrete, if you feed new data into your IBM you'll get different solutions and that's why I told you, what a really dumb idea of mine that was, to think of you as human after all, a person capable of weeping I used to say on those sleepless nights, that's a person I really have to love and respect and of course when you called me up on the phone sounding like a funeral home director I began to suspect it, that there was nothing to be done about it, and maybe you should have let me know about it some other way, let time heal it a little but you're made of other stuff, you wanted to smash the world, wipe out everything that had gone on before and the funniest thing is this idea of yours of putting castling into practice, even though you hate chess; anyway you made a queen's opening gambit here today, there tomorrow you'll have your arms wrapped around someone else and be loving someone else and you'll have moved right along, turned the page and have done with it as easily as saying abracadabra and who gives a damn about someone else's pride, but to call up on the phone and say it like that so coldly I don't love you any more dear and how can anything separate us since nothing unites us, it sounds pretty, doesn't it, but it wasn't like that, the only important thing was that you loved her,

how great, pure Bogart and Clark Gable, love is repaid by love, and
that is just trite, but you're fascinated by trite statements, you practice
the liturgy of words and she's nothing to me any longer you said, and
if I can't live with her otherwise and if she's going to be one of those
who wants to get married first, I prefer to go to hell, and of course,
one of those who wants to get married first, what kind of pride could
distinguish me from her, from that Anastasia Filipovna, than that of
a document signed by a justice of the peace or that of a priest's bless-
ing, you had abandoned me in no man's land, with the child of
nobody in my womb, for me there wasn't any wedding, you got mar-
ried before, you said, and I'm still married to her and then to the
priest for the blessing and the pledge and the holy water and I didn't
have any pride at all left, five years together and all of a sudden I find
out that you hate me, that you've hated me for years, poor little you,
suffering away loving someone else and without saying a single damn
word to me, not a single warning, happy at home with you and in half
an hour you could die of a heart attack, of apoplexy, here today gone
tomorrow, how am I supposed to understand this, you have to excuse
me for not being too smart, for being so thick-headed, my trouble is
that I practice loyalty, what a crazy idea, and besides, right in the midst
of an entire life built up of small daily habits, always assuming I'd see
your familiar expression, the brave look, some gesture of real affection,
but now I understand that it doesn't matter to you at all, that this mat-
ter of a child isn't of the least importance to you, maybe the most
astonishing thing is having lost all fear of death, me who went around
always scared of life, almost not daring to enjoy it because I was so
afraid of losing it, I felt so lucky to have one day after another, with
you at my side, and that gave me enormous strength, even though I
knew right along that it was all a big crapshoot that I could lose or win
like the lottery, but I gave myself up to it far beyond anything reason-
able, the only way to love you was with the total commitment you
wanted, not holding anything back, and I'm made of flesh and blood
after all, you'll see how true that is, five-foot-three and yearning to get
married, I was walking around the world with a guilty conscience even
though just being with you gave me the strength to cut loose from my
bourgeois conventions and all of a sudden that phone call, and that
impersonal voice, and the wedding, blue suit and grey necktie they

said, how amazing, here I am in the middle of my life learning how to deal with being rejected with no clue as to why this had to happen to me, why to me of all people, and it really doesn't matter any more, even though this guy's got me sitting on a filthy old chair, like those out in the country, a chair where there isn't even a crossbar to rest your feet on, oh well, it doesn't really hurt, just the scare of having the anesthetic, but that's because my heart was beating so fast and since I don't have a heart anymore now anyway I can just calm down and then you wake up stretched out on a dirty cot, with a yellowed plastic sheet under you and a grey blanket over you and the world is all blurry and 'atta girl there you go, all done, just wait right here now until the bleeding stops, what a mess, my God, it's running down my legs all sticky and warm, viscous, the truth is that blood is really red, too red, and they make me walk up and down, that's really unpleasant, I can see the nurses grabbing me under the armpits and dragging me up to walk one two, one two, you have to keep walking, you can't drift off to sleep but it would be so nice just to go to sleep, how irritating that they're making me walk up and down this shifting floor, dragging my poor cramped-up legs, and a shot in the butt and rest your head on your knees, I don't want to rest my head on my knees, my knees are too hard, like two old granite blocks, I probably should have gotten someone to come with me, it's so hard to drive along San Diego Street but they aren't letting me leave, that moustached guy in the white apron already told me that, who do you want me to call ma'am, as though there were anyone to call at times like this, the noonday sun is streaming through the window, it's a filthy window with the paint flaking off, I'd like to open it to see what's on the other side and it's impossible to let her fall asleep someone says, and they drag me around the room again they make me stumble back and forth over floorboards that creak and rock up and down, this room keeps growing and shrinking, sometimes I see it as big as a gym I'll never get to the other side, but coming back now one two one two and sitting down again with my head in the lap of an old toothless woman, no teeth, my God how weak I feel, what's happening to me, why, it was probably a little boy, a little girl, maybe it was such a special child this seed you planted in me as a last humiliation and I can't think about those things now, it doesn't make any sense while you're off on your honeymoon in the

Caribbean, I *was only a speck in your eye, dear,* that's my song all right, *and you've wept me* out in a single tear, the old woman is rubbing my neck and I hear her say I'm through the worst of it now, that now I can leave and that I should drink a cup of strong black coffee and a glass of lemon juice, and they're cleaning off my legs with cotton balls, now I'm realizing that they never took off my shoes and I'm squishing along in blood, how disgusting, I'll have to throw them out before I get home and then I have to go out to the street and get into the car and I walk along the sidewalk as though I were floating, it's true, as though my hands were disconnected, as though my head were an immense globe but I'm not afraid, and on the corner I buy a bunch of violets from the florist who looks at me with concern, I'd swear he looks at me with concern and the sun is shining like it does every day and it's Thursday at two o'clock in the afternoon and I get into the car and close the door and I drive along Alameda at sixty and I'd swear that I'm not crying, I swear it, I don't have a single tear in my eyes, what's happening is that the sun is really bothering me, my eyes are stinging a little but that doesn't matter and I floor the gas pedal as though the red lights were all made of the blood of dead babies and I refuse to obey them.

Translated by Mary G. Berg.
From Volume 9: *What Is Secret*

CRISTINA PACHECO

NOODLE SOUP

One P.M.: For more than an hour Luz has been shuttling back and forth between the sink and the stove in the corner. When she's not washing dishes, she's checking the burners to see how the food is doing. She takes a sample from the pot, holds it in the palm of her hand, then tastes:

"The soup's just about ready, so you'll have to head out soon," she says to Josefina, the daughter who will go in her place to deliver dinner to Santos.

Since early this morning, when her husband left for work, Luz has worn the baggy, sleeveless dress that hangs in the front as if she were still expecting. But she's not. Her youngest will soon be two months old. His name is Cruz because he was born on the third of May. During the day the baby sleeps in his parents' bed "so that I can keep an eye on him from here, from the kitchen. At night, I switch him to Lety's crib."

When she finishes grinding the *salsa*, Luz goes back to the stove. She peers into the clay pot and, discouraged, says:

"It looks like you'll have to go without the beans. They're hard as rocks. I hate to buy them around here; everything's so stale," she insists, as she places the lunchbox on the table. "You're getting a late start, so take the Metro. Be very careful crossing the street. You remember where to get off, don't you?"

Josefina listens to her in silence, eyes wide, as if trying to memorize everything her mother tells her.

"Your dad is going to be angry when he sees you; he doesn't like you out on the streets alone, but at this point, there's no choice. Tell him I got hung up waiting for the man who's coming to fix the gas; it's still leaking, even though I plugged the little hole with a chunk of soap. I think I better shut it off as soon as the beans start boiling again because I'm always afraid—the last thing we need is to be blown up."

Luz stops short when she sees her three sons tripping over one another as they enter the kitchen. The boys' restlessness makes her mad.

"As soon as you smell the soup, you decide to show up, right? Bunch of lousy kids!" Rogelio, the oldest, moves toward the stove, anxious to see what's boiling over the flame. "Out of my way, young man. Can't you see that you could knock over the pot? What are you after? I'm cooking beans."

"Ugh, not beans again..."

"Well, what did you expect, angels' breasts or something?"

Dressed in an undershirt that covers only half her body, Leticia appears. She picks up a toy cup she finds on the floor, raises it and says in baby talk:

"Soup, sou...."

"Soup, my foot. First we send a bowl to your father. You be patient, little lady, we'll eat in a minute." Luz feels boxed in by her children and yells at them. "All of you get out of here and go play somewhere else; you don't have to be right on top of me. Josefina, grab two Metro tickets from my pocketbook. And, for the hundredth time, will you put some underpants on your sister? Just look how she's dressed!"

One twenty-five P.M.: As she walks, Josefina is happy to hear the light tap of the lunchbox clasps. She associates the sound with good times: when her father has work and there's food in the house. At "The Parrots," the small stand where the local wiseguys drink, she crosses the street and walks along the riverbank; that way she avoids being brushed by their hands. Even so, she can't help hearing certain comments that make her blush.

Finally, she reaches the subway station. As soon as she steps onto the platform, she feels the crush of the crowd pressing toward the car. In a hurry, she doesn't hesitate to jump aboard just as the doors are about to close. "You almost got caught," says an anonymous voice.

The lunchbox rattles with the motion of the train. The aroma of the food is barely detectable among the many odors that permeate the car. Josefina smiles when a harmless drunk standing next to her says,

"It sure smells good." Someone makes a comment that has a double meaning. People start to move again as passengers who want to get off crowd around the doorway, oblivious to the folks they hit or shove. Josefina doesn't have time to protect herself from the mob, loses her balance, and in an instant sees a small puddle of noodle soup at her feet.

"Geez, you stained my pants," says a man, stomping.

"Move back a bit, we're being crushed."

"Did you spill the whole thing? All of it? What a shame, I could tell it was delicious," says a little old lady dressed in bright colors.

"And with the price of food these days, spilling it... The worst part is that not even a dog can take advantage of it in here."

One fifty-eight P.M.: Josefina doesn't say a word. She just stares at the soup, which has already begun to look repulsive. She stiffly takes the lunchbox cover someone hands her: "It landed way over there." Ashamed, the girl can no longer stand the comments and decides to get off ahead of her stop. On her way to the door, she feels herself slip on a greasy puddle.

Josefina is sad. The clink of the empty lunchbox suffocates her. While she considers whether to climb the stairs and board the Metro headed home, she thinks about Lety, about her brothers waiting for dinner to be served, about her mother, who had to fend them off so they wouldn't eat their father's portion. Fearful of the severe punishment that awaits her, she is more upset to think that today her father will have nothing to eat.

Far from that spot, near the door of the carpentry shop where he works, Santos looks up and down the street. Over and over he asks himself: "What could have happened? Nobody's brought me any food and it's getting very late."

Translated by Nancy Abraham Hall.
From Volume 9: What Is Secret

GIOVANNA POLLAROLO

WHEN WE MEET AGAIN

What did we talk about before? What, I ask, when we had
neither children nor husband nor maid?
When it was not necessary to hide nor embellish a well-placed,
rather expensive mask.
We talked then of the future,
each would dream of that which today she is not
or of what we have become, though different,
of marrying, having children
leaving our prison-like homes,
saying goodbye forever to the nuns,
of postcard lives without dirty clothes
or dishes to do,
of those things we do not dream even in dreams.

Translated by Marjorie Agosín
From Volume 7: *These Are Not Sweet Girls*

Elena Poniatowska

Happiness

Yes, my love, yes I'm next to you, yes, my dear, yes, I love you my
love, yes, you plead with me not to tell you so often, I know, I know,
these are big words, spoken once and for all life, you never call me
love, my paradise, my love, my heaven, you don't believe in paradise
love, yes my love, take care of me, I don't ever want to leave these four
walls, let me stay in your arms, surround me with your eyes, cover me
with your eyes, save me, protect me, love, happiness, don't go away,
look there is that word again, I bump into it constantly, give me your
hand, later you'll say, but I want to feel it now, say it now, look, the
sun, the heat comes in and these tenacious branches from the ivy with
their tiny hard leaves that sneak in through the warmth of the window
and grow in your room and *intertwine* with us, and I need them, I love
them, they bind us together, because, love, I need you, you are need-
ed, that's it, you are needed and you know it, my needed man who
hardly ever says my name, next to you I don't have a name and when
you say this and the other, my name is never present and you reject my
words, happiness, love, I love you, because you are wise and you don't
like to name things, even though happiness is there, *watching*, with its
happy name floating in the air, on top of us, in the twilight of the after-
noon, and if I say its name it vanishes, and then shadows come and I
say to you, love, give me back the light, then your fingertips travel my
body from my forehead to the tip of my toe, along a path selected by
you, examining me, and I lay motionless, on my side, with my back
toward you and you retrace your fingertips along my sides from the tip
of my toe to my forehead, stopping suddenly at my hip and say, you
have lost weight and I think of a skinny horse like the one Cantinflas'
musketeer used when he hung his feather blanket on its bony rump,
because I, my love, I am your old nag, and I can't gallop anymore and
I await you watchfully, yes, I watch you, telling you, don't leave me, you
have nothing to do but to be with me, with your hand on my hip, no,
we won't leave this place, tie me up, put your shirt on me, you laugh

because it looks so big on me, don't laugh, go and get lemonade from
the kitchen because it's hot and we are thirsty, go on, go, no, wait for
me, I'll go, no, I'll go, well you go, wait, don't get up, now it's my turn,
I already went running for the lemonade and I'm here again next to
you, as you lie on the bed, free and naked like dusk, drink some of it,
drink the bright light, don't you realize, I don't want the sun to go
away while we drink happiness, I don't want the sun to go away or for
you to stop stretching out like that, in the timeless afternoon and
evening that come in through the window, our window, look, cover it
with your hand, so the night will stay out, a window should be there
forever, although you can cover the sun for me with a finger, yes, my
love, yes, I'm here, your window to the world, cover me with your
hand, dim me like the sun, you can make the night, you breathe and
the air ceases to flow through the window, how happy we are, look
how warm you are, the window has remained motionless like me, sta-
tic forever, cover me with your hand, Oh! how I forget it all! the win-
dow protects our only exit, our communication with the stars, I love
you, my love, let's go to heaven while the neighbor does the wash in
the yard, in her yard, a laundress's yard, while here in your yard no one
washes and there is wild ivy in the sink, it's tall and the wind makes
it sway because it can't blow clothes on an empty clothesline, you
remember, in October a sunflower grew there, small, emaciated, but I
felt it swirl over my womb, in my tossed hair, disarranged, sad and yel-
low like a small abandoned garden, a tiny garden in the outskirts of
the city climbing through the thatch and coming here and entering
through the window to this house of crumbs, a white bread house,
where I am in the heart of tenderness, a golden house, round as hope,
ring around the rosie, house of happiness, have pity on us, surround
us with your lime walls, don't open your door, don't toss us out in the
open, we have filled you with words, look, look, say again: my love, my
paradise, my paradise, my love, the heat rises and I don't know what
to do anymore to silence my heartbeats and I don't move, you see,
don't say I look like a locust, a grasshopper, don't say I look like a
dressed flea, I don't move any longer, you see, why do you tell me: be
calm, if I'm not doing anything, I only ask you if you want to sleep,
and you bring me close to you, I embrace you and I pin myself to your
mouth like a medal, and I know you don't want to, you don't want to

sleep, you only want us to be still, still and tame while the heat rises from the earth, and grows, throbbing us, I love you, my love, we are the couple, the archetype, I lean against you, I lay my head like a medallion on your chest, I inscribe myself on to you, like a love word coined in your mouth, there are flames on your lips, heat that suddenly melts my being, now on the Pentecost holy day, but we'll never die, right? because no one loves each other as we do, no one loves each other like this because you and I are we and no one is stronger than the two of us, here, locked up in your chest and in mine, let me see you, you are inside of me, look at me with my eyes, don't close them, don't sleep my love, don't go away into sleep, your eyelids are closing, look at me, let me see you, don't leave me, don't let the sun go away, I don't want it to dim, to set, don't yield like the light, the sun, leave everything as it was over my skin, look, you can see me now better than ever because the afternoon is coming to an end, because you are leaving me also, and here I am telling you: don't leave me, be with me forever, strong as the burning sun I stared at as a child with my open eyes, until I saw black, black like the routine ending of fairy tales with the princess living happily ever after with many, many children, don't sleep, don't sleep I'm telling you, anxiously, constantly, with no afterwards, because there is no afterwards anymore for us, even if you leave me, but you'll never leave me, you'll have to come to pick me up, to put the pieces back together once again on the bed and here I am in one piece, and you can't leave me because you would have to return and you would miss a part of me forever, like the missing piece from a puzzle that ruins the entire picture, all the life you had given me and you can't take away from me because you would die, you would go blind and you wouldn't be able to find me limping, crippled, maimed by you, without words, mute, with the word final sealing my lips, the final ending of all stories, there is no longer a story, I don't tell you stories, endings, nothing counts anymore, things get transformed, there's no longer an extra hour on earth, look, the window screen has holes, I can see the two butterflies on the wall with their papier-maché wings, yellow, pink, orange, and the cotton candy and that small wooden bird you bought on the street the Friday everything began, the yellow Friday like the tiny bird black and shocking pink that pecks us ever since, a child's toy, like the paper butterflies that fly round the park until the real ones leave their cocoons, like the ones you crucified in the other room, big ones, with their marvelous blue transparent wings, you pierced them with a pin, one on top of the other, with a pin that hurts me and I asked you how you did it, well, doing it, and you strung up happiness, you petrified it there on the wall, happy, again this word, I repeat it, it comes back, it returns and I repeat it, and you get irritated and you tell me, there goes the donkey off again to the wheat field, to the greedy blossom of happiness, don't you understand, no, I don't understand, help me to pull out the weeds, help me to walk through God's wheat fields pinned down with the needle without the other butterfly, you say now we are all alone pinned down with the needle, without the other butterfly, that no one belongs to anyone, that what we share is sufficient, and enough, and is even miraculous, yes, yes, yes, my love, it's miraculous, don't close your eyes, I do understand, don't be silent, don't sleep, open up and look at me, you're tired and in a short while you'll fall asleep, you'll enter the river, and I'll remain on the bank, the bank we walked together, do you remember, under the eucalyptus, walking to the pace of the river, under the leaves, under the swords of light, I'm open to all wounds, here, I brought you my young spreading womb, I give you my teeth big and strong like tools and I don't feel ashamed of myself anymore, I lie, yes, I do feel ashamed, and I tell all the nuns I like roses with thorns and all, under the black skirts, while they play with their rosaries, and the wind and the light can't vibrate between their legs, leave this place birds of ill omen, get out, tiny threads of life, withered corner cobwebs, full of dust, get out, narrow, half-opened doors, go into mourning, spying crevices, get out brooms, let me sweep the world with all of you, you that swept out so many colored papers from my soul, and you love stay, I wish I had met you when I was older, spinning near the hearth my longings for you, even if you had never arrived, and singing to myself the same old song, when I was young he would fall asleep under my window, even if it weren't true, because now you came early, before I had time to get up, and you put your hand on the slit of the door, and you moved the latch, and I liked your pants with their bulging pockets, your pockets that seem to carry inside of them all of life's accidents, and your own thoughts, like little balls of wrapped caramel candy, your thoughts, tell me, what are you thinking my love? tell me what are you thinking right now, just right now when you stay like this as if you were with yourself, alone, forgetting that I'm here with you, my love, what are you thinking? I always ask the same, do you love me? you're falling asleep, I know you'll fall asleep and I'll get dressed without making a sound, and I'll close the door carefully, to leave you there wrapped in the warm red and ocher of the afternoon, because you have fallen asleep and you don't belong to me anymore and you didn't take me with you, you left me behind, today in the afternoon when the sun and the warm light were pounding through the window, and I am going to walk a lot, a lot, and the neighbor will see me from her door, with her disapproving look because only from time to time do I venture through this path, I'll walk up to the eucalyptus trees, until I'm exhausted, until I accept that you are a sleeping body over there, and that I am another one here walking and that together the two of us are

hopelessly,

hopelessly,

madly,

desperately,

alone.

Translated by Carmen C. Esteves.
From Volume 6: *Pleasure in the Word*

ALFONSINA STORNI

YOU WANT ME WHITE

You'd like me to be white as dawn,
You'd like me to be made of foam,
You wish I were mother of pearl,
A lily,
Chaste above all others.
Of delicate perfume.
A closed bud.

Not one ray of the moon
Should have filtered me,
Not one daisy
Should have called me sister.
You want me to be snowy,
You want me to be white,
You want me to be like dawn.

You who have held all the wine glasses
In your hand,
Your lips stained purple
With fruit and honey,
You who in the banquet
Crowned with young vines
Made toasts with your flesh to Bacchus.
You who in the gardens
Black with Deceit
Dressed in red,
Ran to your Ruin.
You who keep your skeleton
Well preserved, intact,
I don't know yet

Through what miracles
You want to make me white
(God forgive you),
You want to make me chaste
(God forgive you),
You want to make me like dawn!

Run away to the woods;
Go to the mountain;
Wash your mouth;
Get to know the wet earth
With your hands;
Feed your body
With bitter roots;
Drink from the rocks;
Sleep on the white frost;
Renew your tissue
With the salt of rocks and water;
Talk to the birds
And get up at dawn.
And when your flesh
Has returned to you,
And when you have put
Your soul back into it,
Your soul which was left entangled
In all the bedrooms,
Then, my good man,
Ask me to be white,
Aske me to be snowy,
Ask me to be chaste.

Translated by Marion Freeman and Mary Crow.
From Volume 1: *Alfonsina Storni: Selected Poems*

Liliana Heker

When Everything Shines

Everything began with the wind. It all began when Daisy told her husband all about the wind. He hadn't even managed to shut the door to the house. He remained frozen in the position of shutting it, with his arm stretching toward the latch, and his eyes fixed on the eyes of his wife. It seemed like he was going to remain in this perpetual position, until finally, he howled. His reaction was surprising. For several seconds the two remained motionless, studying each other, as if they were trying to confirm in the presence of the other that which had just happened, that is, until Daisy broke the spell. With familiarity, almost with tenderness, as if nothing had happened, she leaned one hand against the arm of her husband in order to maintain her equilibrium while with the other, she pushed the door softly shut and then with her right foot and a felt slipper, removed from the floor the dust that had entered.

"How was your day, dear?" she asked.

And she asked it less out of curiosity (given the circumstances, she wasn't expecting an answer, nor did she receive one) than from a need to reestablish a ritual. She had to communicate with him succinctly by means of her habitual late afternoon question and transmit a message to him. Be that as it may, everything was in order. Nothing has happened. Nothing new can happen.

She finished cleaning the entrance and let go of her husband's arm. He withdrew suddenly toward the direction of the bedroom and left with the impression that a butterfly leaves behind in the fingers, when it frees itself quickly from the one who had held it by the wings. He hadn't used his slippers; this is how Daisy knew that her husband was furious. Without a doubt, he was exaggerating. When all is said and done, she had not asked him to hurl himself nude from the top of the obelisk. With her own slippers, she cleaned the shoe scuffs that he had left behind. However, she did not enter the bedroom: she knew that it was better not to add fuel to the fire. Right at the door, she changed her course and headed to the kitchen; later on she would find a more appropriate moment to talk to him about the wind.

She had just finished preparing supper. At first, so as to please him in spite of it being Wednesday, she had thought about having some steak with French fries, but she quickly changed her mind: vaporized grease saturates the cupboards, it saturates the walls, and even saturates the desire to live; if one leaves it floating around from Wednesday until Monday, which is the day of heavy duty cleaning, the grease has enough time to penetrate to the very pores of things and stay there forever. Therefore, Daisy took a frozen dinner from the freezer and put it in the oven and was setting the table when she heard her husband enter the bathroom. A minute later, like a good omen, the happy hum of the shower echoed through the house.

It was time to go to the bedroom. Daisy barely had entered when she verified that he had left everything in a state of disarray. She brushed his jacket and pants and hung them up, and then she made a little pile out of his shirt and socks and went to the bathroom and knocked on the door.

"I am going to enter, dea,r" she said sweetly.

He didn't answer but sang softly. Daisy took the undershirt and underwear and added them to the little pile. She washed enthusiastically. When she turned off the faucet, she heard him humming the waltz "Above the Waves" in the living room. The storm had subsided.

However, early the next morning, while they were eating breakfast and half-smiling so as to diminish the importance of the episode of the previous day, Daisy mentioned the thing about the wind. It was rather silly, she was ready to admit this, but it would cost so little; wasn't it true? He did not have to think about complicating his life in any way. All she simply asked was that when the wind blew from the north, he enter through the back door that faced south; and when it blew from the south, that he enter through the front door that faced north. A rather whimsical request, if that's how he wished to see it, but it would help her so much, he simply could not imagine. She had noticed that as much as she swept and polished, the floor of the vestibule always filled up with dirt whenever there was a north wind. Certainly, he could enter through anywhere he felt like when the wind blew from the east or from the west. And it wasn't even necessary to talk about the times when there was no wind at all.

"I know you don't think this is important enough to make such an issue over," she said and then giggled.

He stood up and looked as if he were about to give a speech, cleared his throat loudly, almost with pleasure, and then gently stooped over, spit on the floor, recovered his earlier position, and left the kitchen with measured steps.

Daisy remained motionless, staring in vain at the circle of spittle shining in the light of the morning sun, as though it were a tiny being from another planet on the floor of her kitchen. A door shut and opened, some walls rumbled, footsteps resounded through the house, another door shut with a clamoring noise. Daisy's mind barely detected the events. Her entire being seemed to converge on the tiny spot on the floor. *An infectious spot.* A feeling of disgust lightly fluttered around in her head; it expanded like a wave and flooded her thoughts. On the bus when people cough, they spread invisible little drops of saliva, each droplet carrying thousands of germs, how many germs are there in...Thousands of millions of germs shook, jumped with joy and bounced about on the red tile. Mechanically, Daisy took the first thing that she had in her hand: a cloth napkin. Kneeling on the floor, she began to scrub the tile energetically. It was useless: the more she scrubbed, the more the sticky zone stood out like a stigma. Flat germs creeping along like amoebas. Daisy left the napkin on top of the table and went to soak a little sponge in detergent. She scrubbed the tile with the sponge and dumped a pail of water over it. She was about to dry the floor, when she came to a complete stop. Had she gone crazy? Hadn't she used a napkin for...? Good heavens, and to think how easy it is to raise a napkin to the lips. She picked it up with a pointed object and studied it with terror. What could she do now? Washing it did not seem to be very wise; therefore, she filled a pan with water, put it on the stove, and then tossed in the napkin.

She was rubbing the table with disinfectant (the napkin had been in contact with the table for a long time) when the telephone rang. She went to answer it and barely went beyond the door of the bedroom when she noticed something unusual, something that revealed itself to her like a weight hanging over her chest and whose reality she could not confirm until she hung up the phone and opened the closet door.

It was not until then that she found out exactly what had happened: his clothing wasn't there. Very well, he had left, how marvelously fine, was she going to cry because of this? She was not going to cry. Was she going to pull out her hair and bang her head up against the walls? She was not going to pull out her hair, much less bang her head against the walls. Is the loss of a man something that should be lamented? As untidy as they are, so dirty—they cut bread on top of the table, they leave behind scuff marks from their dirty shoes, they open up doors against the wind, they spit on the floor and one can never keep her house clean, the body, one can never keep her body clean either, in the night they are like dribbling beasts, oh their breath and their sweat, oh their semen, the disgusting moisture of love, because my God, You who could do everything, why did You make love so unclean, the bodies of Your children so filled with filth, the world You created so filled with rubbish? But never again. Never ever again in her house. Daisy pulled the sheets off the bed, removed the curtains from their rods, picked up the rugs, removed and dusted and brushed until her knuckles turned red and her arms began to cramp. She washed the walls, waxed the floors, polished the metal, got shimmering lusters from the pans, gave a diamond-like sparkle to the banisters, bathed bucolic porcelain shepardesses as if they were adored children, burnished wood, perfumed closets, whitened opaque surfaces, and polished alabaster figurines. And at seven in the evening, like a painter who puts his signature on a painting that he has dreamt about all his life, she shook the large broom into the garbage can.

She then breathed in deeply the wax-scented air and cast a rather long glance of satisfaction at her surroundings. She captured dazzling lights, savored the whiteness, tasted the transparencies, and noticed that a little bit of dust had fallen out of the garbage can while she was shaking the broom. She swept it up, gathered it with the dust pan and then emptied it into the can. She shook the broom again, but this time with greater care, so that not even a speck of dust would fall out of the can. She put it away in the closet where she was also going to put the pan, when a thought suddenly worried her: people are usually careless when it comes to dust pans; they use them to pick up all sorts of garbage, but it never occurs to them that a little of that garbage must remain stuck to their surfaces. She decided to wash the pan. She covered it with detergent and scrubbed it with a brush while a dark liquid spilled into the sink. Although Daisy let the water run, a black stain still remained at the bottom of the basin. She cleaned it with a sudsy rag, rinsed out the basin, and then washed the rag. Then she remembered the brush. She washed it and dirtied the basin again. She scrubbed the sink with the rag and realized that if she now washed the rag in the sink again, this was going to be an endless business. The most reasonable thing to do was burn the rag. First, she dried it with the hair dryer and then she took it out to the street where she set it on fire. Just as she entered the house, a blast of wind came in from the north and Daisy could not ignore the fact that some ashes had blown into the living room.

It was better not to use the big broom, which was now already clean. She used a small rag with a little bit of wax (because with rags it is always possible to set them on fire). But it was a mistake. The color remained uneven. She polished and spread the wax to an even wider territory; it was all useless!

At about five o'clock in the morning, all the floors of the house were scrubbed, but a red dust still floated in the air, covered the furniture and stuck to the baseboards. Daisy opened the windows, she swept (later on she would find the time to clean the broom and in the worst scenario, she could throw it out) and was finishing the cleaning of the baseboards when she noticed that a little water had spilled. She looked at the water stains on the floor with dismay; she was getting tired, and by the color of the sky it must have been almost seven in the morning. She decided to put this off until later; with luck, she would not have to scrub all the floors again.

She jumped into bed with her clothes on (later she must not forget to change the sheets again) and fell asleep immediately, but the water stains expanded, softened and extended their tentacles. They had trapped her. They were a swamp in which Daisy was sinking fast and furious. She woke up frightened. She had not even slept half an hour. She got up and went to see the stains; they were already pretty dry but they had not disappeared. She scrubbed the area, but it never remained the same color. A light dizzy spell made her fall; she opened her eyes dreamily, vaguely glimpsed the streaks and sighed; she guessed she had not eaten anything in the last twenty-four hours. She got up and went to the kitchen.

A warm meal would perhaps make her feel better, but maybe not—afterward she would have to wash the pots. She opened the refrigerator and was about to take out an apple when a wave of terror invaded her thoughts. She had not swept away the dust settlings and the windows were still open. She withdrew her hand brusquely from the refrigerator and knocked down a little basket of eggs. She watched the yellow viscous puddle spreading slowly. She felt like she was going to cry, but there was no way she was going to do that; one thing at a time. Now, she would sweep away the dust settlings; the kitchen floor would have its turn, nothing like a little bit of order. She looked for the big broom and the dust pan; she went to the living room, and when she was about to start sweeping, she noticed the soles of her shoes. Without a doubt, they were not clean; they had traced a discontinuous path of egg across the parquet floor. Seeing herself with the broom and pan almost made Daisy laugh. *Dust settlings* she murmured, *dust settlings*. She remembered, however, that she still hadn't eaten anything, so she left behind the broom and the pan and went to the kitchen.

The apple was in the center of the yellow puddle. Daisy picked it up, avidly bit into it and suddenly realized that it was absurd not to prepare a warm meal, now that everything was a little dirty. She, therefore, put the pan over the fire, peeled potatoes (it was pleasant letting the long spiral potato peels sink lightly into the yolks and whites, now that everything had begun to get dirty and, in any event, would have to be cleaned much later), put the steak on the grill and the oil in the skillet. The grease sizzled happily, the potatoes sputtered and Daisy realized that she had forgotten to open the kitchen window; be that as it may, it was too late to worry— the vaporized grease had already penetrated her pores and those of other things; it had permeated her clothing and hair and thickened the air as well. The smell of meat and of fried potatoes entered her nasal passages, overwhelmed her and made her go mad with delight.

Impatience can make people a little clumsy. Some oil fell on the floor as she removed the potatoes; she scattered it furtively with her foot, took out the steak and dropped it on the floor. When she picked it up, the closeness, the contact, the marvelous aroma of broiled meat intoxicated her. She could not resist sinking her teeth into it before setting it on the plate.

She ate ferociously. She put the dirty things in the sink but didn't wash them; she was very sleepy, the moment to wash everything would soon arrive. She turned on the faucet so that the water would run and headed toward the bedroom, but she never made it there. Before leaving the kitchen, the oil on the soles of her shoes made her slip, and she fell to the floor. In any event, she felt very comfortable on the floor. She leaned her head against the tiles and fell asleep. The water awakened her. Slightly greasy, it slithered around the kitchen, broke off into subtle streams along the joints of the tiles and, thinning out but persistent, advanced toward the dining room. Daisy had a slight headache. She immersed her hand in the water and refreshed her temples. She turned her head, stuck out her tongue as far as she could, and managed to drink: Now she felt much better. Perhaps she was a little dissheveled, but she lacked the energy to get up and go to the bathroom. Anyway, everything was now quite dirty.

She must not dirty her little dress. Daisy was six years old and she better not dirty her little dress. Not even her knees. She had to be very careful and not get her knees dirty. That is until nightfall, when a voice would shout: time to take a bath! Then she would run frenetically to the back of the house, roll about in the dirt and fill her hair, fingernails and ears with it; she had to feel that she was dirty, that each little corner of her body was dirty in order to be able to later submerge herself in the purifying bath, the bath that would carry away all the filth and leave Daisy as white and as radiant as a flower bud. *Do daisies have flower buds, Mommy?* She felt an indescribable sense of well-being. She moved away a little from the place where she had been lying and felt like laughing. Her finger pointed to a place that was next to her on the ground. Poop, she said. Her finger then sank voluptuously into the excrement, and she wrote her name on the ground. *Daisy.* But it wasn't very noticeable on the red tile. She now got up without much effort and wrote on the wall. *Shit.* Then she signed *Daisy* and drew a big heart around the inscription. A blast of air against her back made her shiver. The wind. It entered through the opened windows, dragged in the dust from the street, dragged in the world's garbage that stuck to the walls and to her name and heart; it mixed with the water that ran into the dining room, entered through her nose, her ears and her eyes and dirtied her little dress.

Five days later, on a luminous sunny day with a glorious blue sky and singing birds, Daisy's husband stopped before a flower stand. "Daisies," said the vendor. "The whitest in the world. Many daisies." With an enormous bunch of flowers, he walked toward his house. Before putting the key in the door, however, he performed a little charade, a roguish act that was filled with love and worthy of being viewed by a loving wife who would be spying behind the sheer window curtains: he sucked his index finger and raising it like a banner, analyzed the direction of the wind. It was coming from the north. The man, therefore, docilely and happily relishing the unequaled taste of reconciliation, went around his house. Whistling a festive song, he opened the door, and a soft, gurgling splatter reached him from the kitchen.

Translated by Celeste Kostopulos-Cooperman.
From Volume 4: *Secret Weavers*

MARTA BRUNET

SOLITUDE OF BLOOD

The base was made of bronze, with a drawing of lacework flowers. The same flowers were painted on the reservoir glass, and a white spherical shade interrupted its extremities to allow the chimney to pass through. That lamp was the showpiece of the house. Placed in the center of the table, on top of a meticulously elaborate crocheted table cover, it was turned on only when there was a dinner guest, an unexpected, remote occurrence. But it was also lighted on Saturday night, every Saturday, because that eve of a worry-free morning could be celebrated in some way, and nothing could be better than to have the lamp spreading its brightness over the vivid tangle of paper that covered the walls, over the china cabinet so symmetrically decorated with fruit plates, soup tureens and formal stacks of dishes; over the doors of the cupboard, with decorative panels and the iron latch, and its lock, speaking of the same time period as the grating that protected the window on the garden side of the house. Yes, every Saturday night the lamplight traced out for the man and the woman a little hollow of intimacy, generally peaceful.

From living in contact with the earth, the man seemed made of telluric elements. In the south, in the mountains, looking at their reflection in the translucent eye of the lakes, the trees, polished by wind and by water, had strange shapes and startling qualities. In that wood worked by the pitiless harsh weather the man was carved. The years had made furrows in his face, and from that fallow field sprouted his beard, moustache, eyebrows, eyelashes. And his tangled mat of hair, coal black, crowned his head with a rebellious shock, which was always escaping over his forehead and which he would push back into place with a characteristic mechanical gesture.

Now, in the brightness of the lamplight, the large hands carefully shuffled a deck of cards. He spread the cards out over the table. Absorbed in the game of solitaire, slow and meticulous, because he was about to win, his features swelled with a kind of pleasantness. He

107

hardly had any cards left in his hand. He drew one. He turned it over and suddenly the pleasantness turned into harshness. He gazed at the cards with rapt attention, the new card in his hand. He put down his remaining cards and tossed the big shock back, sinking and fixing his fingers in his hair. The pleasantness spread over his face again. He lifted his eyelids, and his eyes appeared like grapes, azure-blue. A cautious glance that became fixed on the woman, that found the woman's eyes, grey, so clear, that in certain light or from a distance they gave the unsettling sensation of being blind.

"Just imagine that I'm not looking at you and go on with your trick...," said the woman with a voice that sang.

"Will it turn out really badly?" asked the man.

"If it does, it does."

"It always fails to work for me! Come on, for God's sake! I'll do it again!" And he gathered the cards together to shuffle them

Sometimes the game of solitaire "came out." Other times it "turned stubborn." But always at ten o'clock, the hours resonating in the corridor as they fell from the old clock, the man pulled himself up, looked at the woman, came toward her until he could put a hand on her head, and he caressed her hair, again and again, to conclude by saying, as he said that night: "Until tomorrow, little one. Don't stay up for a long time, be sure the lamp is completely out and don't make a lot of noise with your phonograph. Let me drop off to sleep first..."

He left, closing the door. She heard his long strides through the corridor. Then she heard him go out onto the patio, saying something to the dog, turning around, going back and forth through the bedroom; she heard the bed creak, his heavy shoes falling one after the other, the bed creaking again, the man turning over, becoming quiet. The woman had abandoned the knitting in her lap. She was scarcely breathing, her mouth partially open, her whole self gathering in the sounds, separating them, classifying them, her auditory perception fine-tuned to such a point that all her senses seemed to have been transformed into one big ear. Tall, strong, her naturally brown skin tanned by the sun, she might have been any ordinary creole woman if her eyes had not set her apart, creating a face that memory immediately put in a place all by itself. Tension caused a little bead of perspiration to break out on her forehead. That was all. But she felt her chilled skin and, with an unconscious gesture, passed her hand slowly over it. Then, just as absent-mindedly, she looked at that hand. With every moment she seemed more tense, more like an antenna ready to receive a signal. And the signal came. From the bedroom, and in the form of a snoring sound, which was followed, arhythmically, by others.

Her muscles went limp. Her senses opened up into an exact five-pointed star, each one doing its particular job. But the woman still remained motionless, with her expanding pupils fixed on the lamp.

When had she bought that lamp? One time when she went to the town, when she sold her habitual dozen children's outfits, knitted between one household chore and another, between chores that were always the same, methodically distributed over days that were indistinguishable one from another. She bought that lamp as she had bought the china cabinet, and the wicker furniture, and the wardrobe with the mirror, and the quilted eiderdown comforter. Yes, as she had bought so many things, so much... Of course, over so many years! How many years had it been? Eighteen. She was thirty-six now, and she was eighteen when she got married. Eighteen and eighteen. Yes....The lamp. The china cabinet. The wicker furniture... She never believed, of this she was sure, that by knitting she could earn money not only to dress herself, but to give herself household conveniences.

He said, no sooner had they gotten married, "You have to be enterprising in order to establish your own little business and earn money for your necessities. Raise chickens or sell eggs."

She answered, "You know I'm ignorant about these things."

"Look for something that you know how to do then. Something they taught you in school."

"I could sell candy."

"Give up on selling in this God-forsaken place. It ought to be something that can be carried all together once a month to the town."

"I could knit."

"That's not a bad idea. But it's necessary to buy wool," he added, suddenly uneasy. "How much would you need to get started?"

"I don't know. Let me check prices and ask around in the store to see if people are interested in knitted articles."

"If it doesn't come out being really expensive..."

And it did not turn out to be expensive, and it was definitely a good business enterprise. The wife of the store owner himself bought the first completed item for her son, which was merely a sample. A lovely little suit, such as no child had ever had in that "God-forsaken place," where the people handled money and acquired tasteless things in shops in which the barrel of fat was next to the bottles of perfume and the cheap woolens were next to the medicinal balm. Her business was a big success. People placed orders with her. She knitted for the whole region. She was able to raise her prices. She never had enough supplies for the orders that were pending. When he saw that she was prospering, he said one day, "It's a good idea for you to give me back the ten *pesos* I lent you to begin your knitting. And don't spend all the money that you earn just on things for yourself. Of course I'm not going to tell you to give me this money, it's yours, yes, you've earned it, and I'm not going to tell you to hand it over to me." He always repeated what he had just expressed, insisting, wanting to impress the idea on his own mind. "But now you see, now it's necessary to buy a big kettle and to fix the cellar door. You could easily assume responsibility for the household affairs, now that you have so much money at your disposal. Yes..., so much money."

She bought the big kettle, she had the cellar door repaired. And then, she bought, and she bought...because it represented happiness to her to be converting that mess of a country house, eaten up by neglect, into what it was now, a house like hers there in the north, in the little town shaded by willows and acacias, with the river singing or rumbling down the valley, and the Andes right there, ever present, background for the little houses that seemed like toys: blue pink, yellow, with wide entrance halls and a jasmine bush perfuming the siestas, and facing the patio gate, a painted green bench, inviting casual conversation in the early evening, when the birds and the angelus were taking flight through the skies in the same air, and the peaks took on violent pinks and gentle violet colors, before falling asleep beneath the blanket of watchful gleaming stars.

She closed her eyelids, as if she, too, should fall asleep in the shelter of that vigilance. But she opened them again right away and lis-

tened again, certain of hearing the rhythm of the one who was sleep-
ing. Then she picked herself up and with silent movements opened the
cupboard, and from the highest shelf she went about taking down and
placing on the table an old phonograph, improbably shaped, like a lit-
tle cabinet whose open main doors revealed a set of zither strings at
an oblique angle over the mouth of the receiver, which was nothing
but a small open circle in the sound chamber. Below, other doors,
smaller, afforded a view of the green turntable. That phonograph was
her own luxury item, not like the lamp, luxury of the house, but hers,
hers. Purchased when the señora from "los Tapiales," passing through
the town, had found her in the store and seen her knitted articles and
asked her if she could make some overcoats for her little girls. What a
beautiful woman, with a mouth so large and tender and a voice that
dragged out her "rr's," as if she were a French lady; but she wasn't, and
that really made her laugh. What a workload she had that summer!
That was when she saw fulfilled her longing to have a phonograph
with records and everything. He permitted her to buy it. That was
what she earned all that money for!

"Just buy it, my dear. What's yours is yours, of course, but it would
be good if you could also see about buying a poncho for me, for the
wool flannel one is wearing through. Because the poncho is a real
necessity, and since I have to get together money for another pair of
oxen, it's not a matter of squandering funds, and since you are earn-
ing so much... But it's clear, yes, that you'll buy yourself the phono-
graph too, and before anything else..."

First, she bought the poncho and immediately afterwards the
phonograph. Never greater was her pleasure than being back at home,
the phonograph set up on the table, listening insatiably to the cadence
of the waltz or the march that was abruptly interrupted to let the
sound of tolling bells be heard. They had sold it to her with the right
to two records that she might choose carefully; yet he was impatient on
seeing her indecisive after choosing the first one—which was the one
with the waltz and the march on it—having to try out a whole album
one record after another. Until he said, getting more and more impa-
tient, "It's getting late. Look how the sun is going down. We've got to
go, yes. Night will catch us here if we don't. Take that one that you

have set aside, and this one. One because you like it, and the other let's leave up to chance..." and he pulled out at random a record from the box, which turned out to have Spanish songs filled with laments, which neither he nor she liked and which she tried in vain to exchange. And when, some time later, she hinted timidly at the idea of buying more records, he—with the claylike expression that he was accustomed to wearing when he was being negative—answered severely, "No more fuss in the house. What you've got is enough and with that you can get along."

She never insisted. When she was alone, when he and his laborers were in the field working, she would take out the phonograph and in a standing position, with a vague uneasiness that she was "wasting time"—as he said—her hands together and a spiral of joy beginning to stir in her breast, she let herself sink sweetly into the music.

He did not at all like this "wasting time." She knew this well and did not allow herself to be carried away by the overwhelming desire to hear the waltz or to hear the march. But out of that habit of telling him, in minute detail, whatever she had done during the day, a habit to which he had made her accustomed since the beginning of their married life, she said, her eyelids open and her pupils dilated:

"I ground the flour for the workers, I mended your coat, I kneaded dough for the house..." She paused imperceptibly and added very gently, "I listened to the phonograph for a while and that's all..."

"Wanting to waste time, time that's useful for so many things that bring in money, yes, to waste it..." He said it in different tones of voice, sometimes ascertaining a weakness in the woman, gently protective and condescending; sometimes absent-minded, mechanical, tossing back the rebellious shock of hair, troubled by another idea; sometimes stern, wooden and frightening her, she who had never been able to prevail over a dark, instinctive submissiveness of female animal to male, who in former years humiliated herself to her father and in the present, to her husband.

When she, without any hinting, bought that leather jacket for him—shiny as if it were waxed, black and long, which the storekeeper said was for a mechanic and which the rain could not seep into, like that which might fall in the stubborn downpours of the region—when she bought it and mysteriously brought it home and left the package in front of his place at the table—so that he might find it by surprise—the man, his mood softening on seeing it, passed his big hand over her soft hair, done up in braids and raised like a tiara on her head.

"You're a good old gal. Hard-working, like women ought to be, yes. And listen, little one, tonight since its Saturday, light the lamp, and that way I can do my solitaire better. And when I go off to bed, you'll stay for a little while longer and play your phonograph. Yes, you'll play it, but when I'm sound asleep. You should have your pleasure too..."

Thus, the custom was born. She lowered the lamp's light a little. She went on tiptoes to the window and opened it, letting in the night and its silence. She went back to the table, carefully wound up the phonograph, put her hands together and waited.

Ta-ta, ta-ta, ta-ta-dum...

The march. And suddenly everything around her was blotted out; it disappeared, submerged in the stridency of the trumpets and the roll of the drums, dragging her back through time, until leaving her in the plaza of the northern town after eleven o'clock mass on a rainless Sunday, the drum major spinning the baton around and following after him, marching in step, the band taking the final turn along the parade route, with the children swarming in front, and a dog mixed in among their racing feet, while the ladies on their traditional bench commented on petty problems, the gentlemen talked about the wine harvest, and they—she and her sisters, she and her friends, arm in arm, with their braids uneasily sliding over breasts that were already swelling with sighs—passed and passed again in front of the grown-ups, crossing through groups of boys, who seemed not to see them, and on fixing their gaze on their surroundings only looked at one of them, absorbing them as if thirsty for fresh water, from a real spring, mouths avid, grown large with desire.

It was the occasion when new clothes were shown off. Sometimes they were pink or celestial blue. Sometimes they were red or sea-colored, and this meant that throughout a sky of faded blue a few clouds shed their fleece and that the wind had carried away the last leaf of dark gold. She particularly remembered a red overcoat, with a round collar of white fur, curly and soft against her face and a muff like a little barrel, hanging from the collar by a cord, also white. And the warning from the mother:

"Put your hands in the muff and don't you take them out again. Of course, you can say hello to people...," she added after a thoughtful pause.

They went back and forth, arm in arm. They whispered incomprehensible things, inaudible confidences that drew their heads together, murmurs scarcely articulated that suddenly shook them in long bursts of laughter that left the trees perplexed because it wasn't nesting season, or they stirred the trees to nod approvingly during that other time of year when the birds tried to add their own comments to those musical sounds. Sometimes, no, once, she raised her face to better catch the laughter that always seemed to fall on her from above, and from this foreshortened perspective her pupils found the gaze of a pair of green eyes, as green as new grass and in the face of a boy darkened by the sun, strong and like a freshly sprouting field. Only an instant. But an instant to be carried home and treasured and placed in the depths of her heart, and to feel that a pang of anguish and a feeling of warmth and a vague desire to cry and pass soft fingertips over her lips suddenly tormented her, in the middle of reading, a chore, or a dream. To see him again. To have the feeling impressed on her again that life was stopping in her veins. For that second in which the green gaze of the boy fixed on her was the reason for her existence. Who was he? Was he from the town? No. Someone familiar? No. Perhaps a summer vacationer from a nearby area. She guarded her secret treasure. She talked less, she rarely laughed. But her pupils seemed to become enlarged, to flood her face in that search for the vigorous silhouette, dressed as the boys from the town did not dress. He arrived in a tiny car. It left him beside the club. He went to mass. She observed him from a distance, attentive and circumspect, in the presbytery, a little on the fringe of the group of men. When mass was over, he went to the candy store, filled the car up with packages, then took a walk around the plaza in order to go to the post office, retraced his steps, got into the car and left.

It was obvious that the other girls had noticed him. And dying of laughter over what he was wearing, in his golf or riding pants, they

called him "Baggy Pants," to her hidden desperation.
The march continued filling the house with harmonious sounds.
The bells burst in, as if pealing. Like on certain Sundays, when there
was High Mass; but these were more sonorous bells, more harmo-
nious, as if while they were pealing, pulsations of untapped joy were
mixed with them.
The march ended. She shifted the needle, wound it again, turned
the record over, and now the waltz began to spin around the table,
music that seemed to be dancing, a beat that created soap bubbles,
sometimes slowly, sometimes rapidly, radiating their colors.
She never found out what his name was, who he was, where he was
from. One Sunday he didn't appear. Or the next. Or any other. A
young girl raised the point, "I wonder what's become of 'Baggy Pants'?"
"*La Calchona*, the Witch, has probably eaten him up," answered
another, and they burst out laughing.
Her chest ached, and the sharp claw of sorrow dug at her throat.
The corners of her mouth drew taut, and her eyes, like never before,
filled her face. Once in the house, she sought out the most secluded
corner, in the storage room, between the piano box and a pile of mat-
tresses, and there she released her sorrow, she opened her heart, allow-
ing her pain to escape and envelop her in its viscous mantle, adhering
to her like new skin, moist and painful. The tears rained down her
face. Never to see him again. The sobbing became stronger. What gaze
was going to hold that magic for her? That burning that raged within
her, she did not know where, as if waiting longingly for some unknown
happiness. His name? Enrique...Juan...José...Humberto... And if his
name was Romauldo, like her grandfather's? It did not matter. She
would always love him, whatever his name was... She would love him...
Love him... Love him the way a woman loves, because she already was
a woman and her fifteen years were ripening in her budding breasts,
bringing a downy softness to her intimate zones and giving her voice
a sudden dark tremolo. She would love him forever. She seemed to dis-
integrate into weeping. And suddenly she became still, sighing and
still, without tears, her sorrow diluted, formless and distant. She
sighed again. She wiped her eyes. And she found herself thinking that
probably they were looking for her all over the house, that she ought

to go wash her tear-stained face, that... Yes, it was shameful to confess it, but she was hungry. And she went out gently from among the stored items, watching carefully in order to leave without being seen and to go refresh her face in the courtyard water tank. Her mother stared at her occasionally, seeming confused, and would murmur repeatedly, "What a woman my little girl's become."

The father was more definitive in his conclusion and said at the top of his voice, "Look, Maclovia, we have to marry this one off as soon as possible."

For years she wept her sorrow between the piano box and the stack of mattresses. Nobody ever found out anything. They lifted up her braids, which since then she wore like a tiara around her head. They lowered the hems of all her dresses. No one said that she was pretty. But there wasn't a man who did not become startled on seeing her, lost in the contemplation of her grey eyes, experiencing something akin to vertigo in the presence of her mouth, fleshy, intensely red. Her manner was courteous and indifferent. She had to protect her memory, to keep her dream-fantasy safe, and only in a land of silence could she do this. Men looked at her, they stopped right next to her, but all of them, unanimously, went after other girls who were more accessible to their courtship.

The father introduced the future husband one day. He was from lands to the south, proprietor of a ranch, part of the estate of an old family in the region. Already an older man, of course not a "veteran"; this is what her mother said. As she also added, "A good catch."

Indifferent, she allowed them to interpret her acquiescence among themselves and they married her off. This man or another, it made no difference to her. For not a one of them was hers, the one she loved, that green gaze that filled her blood with tenderness. This one? The other one? What did it matter? And she had to get married, according to what her mother said, smiling and persuasive, and according to what her father ordered with his thundering voice that did not accept dissenting opinions.

She remembered the discomfort of her bridal gown, the crown that pressed against her temples and her terrible fear of ripping the veil. The groom whispered, "It was so expensive, be careful with it..."

The waltz ended. For a moment silence filled the house, a silence so complete that it was injurious. Because it was so complete, the woman began to sense the presence of her heart, and terror forced open her mouth, and then she heard the panting sound of her breathing. But she also perceived the snoring in the other room, broken off when the music was interrupted and which a soothed subconscious mind imposed again upon the sleeping man. Then she heard a cricket in the courtyard. She raised herself up slowly and looked outside at the black and spacious field that she knew was flat, without anything in the distance but the ring of the horizon. Flat. A plain. And in the midst of it, she and her vigil, intercepting memories, caressing the past. Lost on the plain. With no one for her tenderness, to look at her and kindle within her that passion that had moved through her blood before and made her mouth shudder under the trembling touch of her fingers. Alone.

She went back to the phonograph. She would have liked to repeat the magical experience. To spread out again the melodic canvas in order to project the images there once more. But no. The clock struck once. Ten thirty. If he were to wake up...

With the same caution as someone who handles living, fragile creatures, she put away the phonograph and the records, she closed the cupboard, and she put the key in her pocket. From the china cabinet she took out a small match and lit the candle.

Then she turned off the lamp. And she went out to the corridor, following after the light's mysterious glow, pursued by nightmarish shadows impinging on one another.

When she carried the rice pudding to the dining room, she believed she had made the last trip of the evening and that then she could sit down to wait for the guest to leave. But the two men, the lamp between them, dug in their spoons happily, like children, and once they had cleaned their plates, they both raised their heads and sat staring at her, eagerly, their mouths watering.

"Serve yourselves a little more," she said, bringing the platter up beside them.

"Of course, *patrona*; it's really a pleasure to eat this!" admitted the guest.

"It's that the old gal has a good hand for these things!" And the man added in a confidential manner, because the wine was spreading through his body, "Things that they taught her in school; it's worth the trouble to have an educated wife, friend; yes, I'm telling you, and believe me."

She waited, uncomfortable in her chair, her hands placed politely on the tablecloth. During the day they had eaten abundantly from a side of beef and the wine in the big jug was almost gone. It would be a matter of waiting around for awhile for the obligatory after dinner conversation and then the guest would leave. For his house was far away and the night was becoming windy, and over a background of pale stars enormous threatening clouds were creating shapes and then destroying them.

The man's voice caught her attention. "And that coffee? Hurry, for the train won't wait..." And he laughed at his statement, hitting the table with his fist and making the lamp wobble back and forth.

Her trips to the kitchen weren't over. She went out to the corridor thinking, disheartened, that the fire was probably already out and to revive it was a task that would take awhile. But under the ashes the red throbbing of the embers made her almost smile, and the water promptly boiled, and the coffee pot, important-looking with its two tiers, was on the tray, and she was once again walking through the darkened house, for the light of the reflector only seemed to thicken the blackness in the corners.

In the dining room the two men deliberated, sparing their words, their creole sullenness still in effect because that meal was designated to close a deal for the purchase of some pigs that the guest had come from the town to see, and the afternoon had been spent in calculations, "I'll ask for this and offer you that," and they still were not arriving at anything concrete.

"On Monday I'll send you a messenger with the answer," said the guest.

"It's that tomorrow, Sunday, I have to give an answer to one of the parties that's also interested, and I can't put it off any longer, you understand, certainly; it's not good to just leave him waiting and to have him back out and you, too, and I lose a good buyer."

"It's that you insist on such prices."

"What the pigs are worth, friend; you won't find any better ones. There's not another litter like this anywhere around here, as you well know, yes."

The woman had brought out the cups, the sugar; now she served them the coffee. Let them settle their business quickly and have the guest be on his way! And she sat down again, in the same position as before, so identical to, so like, a cardboard cut-out and placed there, so erect, inexpressive and mysterious that suddenly, the two men turned around to look at her, as if attracted by the ecstatic force that emanated from her.

The guest said, "The *patrona* is so quiet!"

And the man, vaguely uncomfortable without knowing why, replied, "Serve some *aguardiente*, then."

She got up again, but this time not to go to the kitchen. She opened the cupboard and stood on her tiptoes to reach up above her the bottle that was stuck away in a corner behind the phonograph. The guest, who was watching her do it, asked solicitously, "Do you want me to help you, *patrona*? The bottle is pretty high up for you."

"Look at it, how troublesome the bottle is, just like a woman. But that's what I'm here for, yes..." exclaimed the man, and he reached up to take it down.

His hands bumped into the phonograph, and he added, delighted to find another token of respect to offer the guest, "Let's tell the *patrona* to play the phonograph for us a little. I call it 'her noisemaker' because you've got to see how it squawks; but she likes it and I let her get her pleasure out of it. That's the way I am, yes. Play something for my friend to hear. Put on what's prettiest. But first you'll serve us something, yes..."

He placed the bottle and the phonograph on the edge of the table. The woman had remained quiet, listening to what the man was saying. But when the big hands seized the little cabinet, a kind of resentment began to stir in her breast, slowly, hardly at all at first. The phonograph was her own property and nobody had any right to it. Never had anyone operated it, except for herself with her own hands, which were loving, as if for touching a child. She swallowed hard and then clenched her teeth, revealing the hard edge of her jaw, just like her father's and just like that of the distant grandfather who had come from the Basque Country. She thought that the *aguardiente* would make them forget the music and instead of the little glasses, green and deceiving, into which a thimbleful of liquid hardly fit, she set out the other big wine glasses and filled them halfway. The men sniffed the *aguardiente*, then raised their eyes at the same time as they clinked the glasses, and in unison said, "To your health!"

And they emptied their contents in one gulp.

"This is *aguardiente!*" the man said.

The guest answered with a whistle that seemed to get stuck in his puckered mouth, a gesture of stupor because something was beginning to dance in his muscles without any intervention of his will, and this left him in this state, perplexed and so happy on the inside.

"Let's talk about the deal again," the man proposed. "It's a good idea now to get it decided, yes; my price is reasonable, as you well know, and you know you're getting pigs that'll bring double the price, yes; fattened up in the feed pen and the boar almost purebred, outstanding pigs for ham..."

The other man smiled leisurely and nodded his assent.

"It's a deal, then?" asked the man. "It's a deal?"

"The *aguardiente's* good; one doesn't drink any better around here, not even in the Pineiros' hotel."

It was strange what he was feeling: still, that sort of muscular movement that now was polarizing in his knees and was hurling his legs in every direction, irreducibly, just like a clown. And he was so happy!

"Good *aguardiente*, of course, yes...; it's a gift from my father-in-law, who's from the vineyard region and he trades in wines. Of the best quality. The deal is set?"

"What deal?" he asked stupidly, attentive to his desire to laugh, to the impossibility of his laughing and to the disconsolate feeling that was beginning to inundate him. And his legs under the table dancing, dancing...

"The deal about the pigs, yes..."

"Oh! Really... But wasn't the *patrona* going to play the...how did you call it...the...well...the phonograph?"

The woman hated him with a violence that might have destroyed him on becoming tangible. All the bad words that she had heard in her existence, and that she never said, suddenly came to her memory and they felt so alive to her that she was astonished they did not turn around to look at her, terrified and speechless in the face of this rude avalanche.

"It's a deal?"

"Music, music...life is short and one must enjoy it..."

But instead of reaching her hand out to the phonograph, the woman had extended it toward the bottle and again she served them, causing the wine glasses to overflow. And since each one, absorbed in his own thoughts, had not seen that the glass had been set in front of him, it was she who said, suddenly cordial, "Serve yourselves!" And she made an inconclusive gesture of invitation, a kind of greeting that stayed in the air, paralyzed, while she watched them drink: "To your health!" And the hoarse sound of her voice saying the toast surprised her.

"It's a deal?" insisted the man, his tongue tangled in his consonants.

The other man did not hear a thing but only felt the tide of distress growing, at the same time as in his ears a cicada began its steady mid-afternoon sawing. And why were his legs dancing?

"Brother, I'm a good man. I don't deserve this..." And the distress spilled over into a hiccough. "I don't want my legs to dance, my legs are mine, mine...Music....," he shouted suddenly and he got up halfway, but he lost his momentum and fell down on top of the table.

The woman watched them, silent, with her eyes so open and inexpressive, so bright, so enormous in their greyness. They were not to come near her phonograph again, they were not to have it; it was hers; therein resided her inner life, her deliverance from colorless days. Outwardly, she was similar to the plain, flat, with her husband's will cutting her level like the wind; but just as the current of water in all its forms passes under the layers of the earth, so she had within herself her singing water saying things from the past. The music belonged to her. To her, and pity anyone who came near it!

But the guest extended a heavy hand and placed it on the little doors of the phonograph, trying to open them. But he did not open them because she, standing up violently and grabbing his hand harshly, said, also harshly, "No. It's mine."

The guest looked at her, with his mouth curled up and trying to think some thought that he had just forgotten. Suddenly he remembered. And again he stretched out the hand that she had removed from the little door latch.

"I'm telling you, no!"

"Look how she's insulting me, brother..."

The man insisted greedily, "It's a deal?"

"Music...," answered the guest, stubbornly.

"Why don't you play something? Go ahead and raise a ruckus, little one, yes; something you like. Don't you see that we're going to close the deal?"

He would not put his hands on the phonograph. Not that, never. The guest had picked himself up and this time his muscles did obey him. But the woman prevented the attack and put herself in between, defensively. The other man reeled about the dining room until, bumping into the wall, he turned around, inflamed with a criminal impulse, blinded to everything that was not his own idea.

"Music...music..."

"Has she gone crazy? What's happening to her?" asked the man.

The guest was on top of her and she on top of the phonograph, defending it with her whole body. They struggled. The man looked at them for an instant, stunned, repeating, "Has she gone crazy? Has she gone crazy?"

But when the guest gave a sharp cry because the woman's teeth were ripping into his hand, he rushed forward to separate them, to defend his friend, to defend his transaction, his deal already almost completed.

She kicked and bit them, behaving like an animal, furious, the way a puma in the wild might defend her cubs. The men did not know why they were getting punched, why they were rolling on the floor, why the table was reeling and the lamp was shifting its light back and forth in a swaying movement that was worse than the sensation in their stomachs. The phonograph fell with a crash and the strings reverberated, like the lament of a grove of trees whose leaves are ripped off by a strong wind. The guest was sitting on the floor, bewildered, and suddenly his cry broke into sobs that interrupted his hiccoughs. The man leaned against the window, astonished by everything and looking at the woman, her clothing in shreds, the magnificence of her hairdo undone, with a long slash on her face, cleaning herself off with the apron that was red with blood, her blouse stained, stubbornly intent on gathering from the floor the pieces of the broken records, looking at them and sobbing, cleaning the blood off herself, sobbing and looking for more pieces and cleaning off the blood and sobbing.

But the guest diverted his attention with his enormous hiccoughs. "Brother, I thought I was in the home of a brother. I've been insulted...I have...," he lamented, stumbling as he spoke.

"Don't cry anymore, brother." And suddenly back to his idea and full of solicitude and tenderness: "It's a deal?"

"Swine, that's just what you are: swine...," shouted the woman, and with her armload of pieces she left the dining room, closing the door with a resounding bang that startled the rats in the loft and caused the dog to gaze at her steadily, its sequin eyes sparkling in the gloom.

* * *

Outside, the wind's mane was whipping about, unleashed in a frenetic gallop. The clouds had pressed themselves tightly together, dense and black, imparting a dark tint to the environs and not allowing the outline of a single thing to be seen, as if the elements had not yet been set apart. A cricket was giving witness, immutably, to its existence.

She fled, pressing the shattered records against her chest as she went, feeling the flow of the blood through the wound, warm and sticky on her neck, making its way inside to the fine skin of her chest. She walked with her head down, breaking through the blackness and the wind. She walked. The house was far away, not just erased by the darkness. The cricket, imperceptible, was left behind, tenaciously useless. She could be out on the plain and be the living center of her desolate surroundings; she could be in a valley bounded by rivers and precipices; she could walk, walk, endlessly, until she fell exhausted upon the hard earth, being grown over evenly with identical weeds; she could suddenly slide down the slope of the ravine and go crashing onto the smooth stones of a river engorged with reddish sand; she could. . . Anything could happen in this blackness of chaos, confusing and dreadful. For to her nothing mattered.

To end it all. To die against the earth. To be destroyed in the ravine. Not to feel anymore that corrosive ardor, bitter to her mouth and clawing around inside her. To end it all. Not to make an effort any more to know what characteristic a certain day had, stubbornly persisting in extracting from the blurry sum a date to differentiate it. Not to live like a machine amidst the daily shuffle and the knitting, longing for Saturday to come in order to eat the crumb of memories that was incapable of satiating her heart's craving for tenderness. To put an end to the sordidness surrounding her, with its disguise of "do as you wish, but...," of meticulousness, of concealed vigilance. To be no more. Never again to return to the house and find herself reporting what she had done and what it had yielded, listening to the insinuation regarding what had to be bought and what needed to be earned. To not get calluses on her hands pounding wheat, neither with her eyes weepy from the smoke of the oven, nor feeling her midsection aching in front of the laundry tub. Never to take pains with painting a little board and making a shelf, nor wallpapering the rooms, bedecking them with flowers like an imitation garden. Never. Nor ever again to feel him heaved over on top of her, panting and sweaty, heavy and without awakening any sensation in her other than a passive repugnance. Never.

The injury, which the air was turning cold, ached like a long stab wound. She touched it and found within the blood a hard point. A piece of glass. A spike-sized sliver from a broken glass that had buried itself there during the struggle, she did not know when. With a sort of insensitivity to the pain, she wiggled it to pull it out. She let out a groan. But furious with herself, in an abrupt tug that ripped her flesh more deeply, she pulled it out and tossed it away.

The blood was running through her fingers, around her neck, over her breasts. All stained and sticky, she kept going. To vanish. But first to sob, to shout, to howl. The wind, with its gusts, seemed to push its way inside her through her open flesh and make the pain intolerable. Greater still, sharper than the other pain which was destroying her feeling. Suddenly the hand that was gripping the apron, still holding the broken records, opened up and everything tumbled out over the ground. She took a few more steps and then fell face down sobbing, the sounds of which the wind seized with its strong hand and scattered throughout the surrounding area.

It was as if the water of those clear eyes could at last be water. She had the sensation that her mouth was opening for her, and she felt the strange noises being hurled from her throat and the scorched eyelids and wrinkled forehead and the salt from her weeping. And a hand clutching the wound, violently painful, and the blood running between her fingers and a braid of hair that must surely be soaked through and dampening her back. She raised herself up on one elbow; she turned her head. And she gave a sharp cry because a breath made her face feel warm and something inhuman terrified her to the point of losing consciousness.

The dog alternated periodically between sniffing her noisily, licking her hands, and sitting down—with his head raised on high, his snout stretched out toward mysterious omens—to deliver a long howl to the moon. He licked her face when the woman came to, and she knew instantaneously that it was the dog, although she did not know where she was. She sat up suddenly, and also suddenly she remembered her immediate situation.

It was as if she had not lived it. So strange, so alien to her. Almost like the sensation of the nightmare that had just become submerged in her subconscious. Was she fleeing from a dream; was she returning from some reality? A movement, on trying to stroke the dog, who was circling around her uneasily, gave her the exact shape of the facts. She groaned and the dog sought out her face again. But she pushed it aside, forcing it to lie down beside her. She pressed on the wound, which was oozing blood again, burning her as if she were being scalded.

She could bleed to death. To remain as she was, still in the night, in the cordial proximity of the dog until her blood went draining away and with it her life, that abhorrent life that she did not want to preserve for the benefit of another. Death would avenge her constant state of humiliation, the animosities that had accumulated wordlessly, the

125

resentment of a frustrated existence. To remove herself from the midst of things so that solitude might be the punishment for the man who would not have anyone to work, to produce and give an accounting of deeds and thoughts; the machine for his pleasure would have vanished and he would have to pay dearly to find another one so perfect as she. Not to see him again. Never to put in front of him the medium-done meat and see him chew with his surprisingly white teeth. Nor to see his gaze becoming clouded over, when desire made him reach out his hand to her futilely elusive body. Not to know that he was tangled up in subterranean calculations: "You'll buy this because this little sum of money is to be stashed away and used to buy, whenever possible, the Urriolas' field, who are deep in debt and will finally have to sell, yes; or the field belonging to Valladares' widow, who with so many kids is not going to prosper, and they're going to put it up for auction, for the mortgage payments..." Waiting like a vulture, patiently, for the moment to take off with the prey. Land. Everything in him was reduced to that. To sell. To negotiate. To bring in money. And buy land, land.

To be no more. To think no more. To feel how the blood was slipping away through her fingers, running stickily over her chest, collecting in her lap, dampening her thighs.

The dog whined softly now, more and more restless. The woman, all of a sudden, opened her eyes, which no longer held any water other than that of their own clear irises, and she came face to face with a truth: to die was also never again to take out the memories of the past, that treasure chest with its images of tenderness. Never again to remember...To remember what? And in a rapid and incoherent super-position of images, snatches of scenes, fragments of sentences, she saw her mother sitting in front of the big gate, she saw herself with her sisters arm in arm, she saw the doves flying through the fragrant air of the garden. She perceived so exactly the smell of the jasmines that she inhaled longingly. But other images appeared: herself crying between the piano box and the pile of mattresses; herself silent in the night under the moon's medallion in the bottom of the water tank; herself in front of the mirror, pinning a sprig of basil and some carnations into her braids because Easter was an obstinately hopeful time; herself with her face turned around by the laughter and her eyes snaring the green gaze that stirred up a timid pigeon in her chest, so warm, so tender, so absolutely alive, that the surprise for her hand was not finding it sweetly nested there... All of that, never again. To die was also to renounce all of that.

Suddenly she stood up. Her legs felt unstable and little particles were dancing before her eyes. She closed them tightly. She forced herself to hold herself erect. She pressed the apron firmly to her face, for she did not want the blood to flow through the wound, for she did not want the blood to abandon her, for death to leave her like an outspread rag in the middle of the field, on top of the mustard weeds, abandoned in the blackness with only the dog's protective custody. She wanted life, she wanted her blood, the branchwork of her blood, laden with memories.

She pressed the apron even harder against her cheek. She stared keenly into the night. Then she called the dog. She took it by its collar. And she said, "Let's go home," and she followed it into the darkness.

Translated by Elaine Dorough Johnson.
From Volume 3: *Landscapes of a New Land.*

MARJORIE AGOSÍN

MY STOMACH

Naked as in silence
I approach my stomach.
It has been changing like a summer
moving away from the sea,
or like a dress that grows wider by the hour.
My stomach
is more than just round,
because when I sit
it spreads out like a
flame,
then,
I touch it to remember
everything in it:
the salt and the happiness,
the winter's fried eggs
the milk I couldn't swallow in my youth,
the Coca-Cola that stained my teeth
the homesickness for a glass of wine
or a dish of potatoes fried in olive oil.

And in remembering,
I feel how it grows
and reaches each time more
ceremoniously for the ground,
it's even affectionate with my feet and my toes
that could never have belonged to a princess.

I rejoice
in having a stomach as wide as the
hats my grandmother wore

in summer.
This Sunday, the seventh,
at seventy-seven years of age,
my stomach
is still my own,
and proudly promenades along the seashore.
Some say I am old and ugly now,
that my breasts are mistaken for my gut
but my stomach, here by my side, keeps me company,
and it is not fat that's overflowing,
only bits of flesh baking under the sun.

Translated by Daisy C. DeFilippis.
From Volume 6: *Pleasure in the Word*

Rosario Castellanos

Speaking of Gabriel

Like all guests my son disturbed me
occupying a place that was mine,
there at the wrong time,
making me split each mouthful in two.

Ugly, sick, bored,
I felt him grow at my expense,
rob my blood of its color, add
a secret weight and volume
to my condition upon this earth.

His body begged mine for birth, to yield to his,
to give him a place in the world,
the provision of time necessary for his history.

I consented. And when he departed through that wound,
through that unloosening hemorrhage,
the last of my aloneness, of my looking from behind a glass
flowed out.
I remained open, manifest
to visitations, to wind, to presence.

ORIGIN

I am growing on a woman's corpse,
my roots wrap themselves around her bones
and from her disfigured heart
a stalk emerges vertical and tough.

From the being of an unborn child:
from her womb cut down before the harvest
I rise stubborn, definitive,
brutal as a tombstone and sad at times
with the stony sadness of the funeral angel
who hides a tearless face between his hands.

Translated by Magda Bogin.
From Volume 7: *These Are Not Sweet Girls*

ILKE BRUNHILDE LAURITO

GENETRIX I

In the beginning was the Womb.

The dark breast fed the world
and darkness conceived the pre-dawn day.

And then came light.

And the sea became an embryo of fish,
the air, a germination of birds.
The earth, on different gestating levels,
fertilized as flower, fruit, reptile, and beast.

In the gravitation of space,
the Sun:
an egg on fire.

GENETRIX III

SHE:
An animal with smooth skin,
without scales or feathers
But with hands and legs.

Between feet and forehead,
the fertile trunk
fructifying thighs,
buttocks
breasts.
In the middle
of the thick forest,
in a covered
cave
the beast awaits.

GENETRIX V

Open sky: the ceiling.
The floor–the earth's ground.
Four architectural winds
of walls and foundations.
The house (the universe).
A small volcano
in the middle of the clearing.
Around her
the domestic animals
warm themselves
and SHE
falls asleep
with a docile snake
intertwined between her legs.

GENETRIX VI

"It is not good for you to be alone,"
crackles
the fire's voice

AND SHE
Perceives in her dream
a strange animal,
in her image and likeness
(but of shallow chest,
and unexpected protrusions)

There was the snake
—the same, only violent—
furious prisoner
between the tense thighs,
rigid and ready to leap
with is effective poison.

Translated by Paula Milla-Kreutzer.
From Volume 6: *Pleasure in the Word*

Rosario Castellanos

On the Edge of Pleasure

I

Between myself and death I've placed your body:
so that its fatal waves might break against you without touching me
and slide into a wild and humiliated foam.
Body of love, of plenitude, of fiestas,
words the winds disperse like flowers,
bells delirious at dusk.
All that the earth sends flying in the form of birds,
all that lakes store up of sky
along with the forest and the stone and the honeycomb.

(Heady with harvests I dance above the haystacks
while time mourns its cracked scythes.)

City of fortune and high walls,
circled by miracles, I rest in the enclosure
of this body that begins where mine leaves off.

II

Convulsed in your arms like a sea among rocks,
breaking against the edge of pleasure or gently
licking the stunned sands.
(I tremble beneath your touch
like a tensed bow quivering with arrows
and sharp imminent hisses.
My blood burns like the blood of hounds
sniffing their prey and ravage.
But beneath your voice my heart surrenders

---

in devoted and submissive doves.)

III

I taste you first in the grapes
that slowly yield to my tongue,
conveying their select, intimate sugars.

Your presence is a jubilation.

When you leave, you trample gardens and turn
the turtledove's sweet drowse
into a fierce expectation of wild dogs.
And love, when you return
my raging spirit senses you draw near
as young deer sense the water's edge.

Translated by Magda Bogin.
From Volume 6: *Pleasure in the Word*

SECTION III
THE POLITICS OF DOMINATION

Emma Sepúlveda-Pulvirenti

September 11, 1973

Santiago, Chile

We shall overcome!
I heard at eight
we shall overcome!
I heard again
at nine

and at ten
and at eleven
and all
the hours
in the petrified day

after

the voices

lowered

weakened

folded

and the silence

devoured the echo

echo
        echo

echo
echo
echo

without me realizing
it became
the sound
of bullets
against the body
of those who rose in opposition.

No

No,
no
not
numbers.
They are not numbers.

They are names.

Translated by Shaun T. Griffin and Emma Sepúlveda-Pulvirenti.
From Volume 7: These Are Not Sweet Girls

Marjorie Agosín

The Most Unbelievable Part

The most unbelievable part,
they were people like us
good manners
well-educated and refined.
Versed in abstract sciences,
always took a box for the symphony
made regular trips to the dentist
attended very nice prep schools
some played golf...

Yes, people like you, like me
family men
grandfathers
uncles and godfathers.

But they went crazy
delighted in burning
children and books
played at decorating cemeteries
bought furniture made of broken bones
dined on tender ears and testicles.

Thought they were invincible
meticulous in their duties
and spoke of torture
in the language of surgeons and butchers.
They assassinated the young of my country
and of yours
now nobody could believe in Alice through the Looking Glass
now nobody could stroll along the avenues

without terror bursting through their bones

And the most unbelievable part
they were people
like you
like me
yes, nice people
just like us.

Translated by Cola Franzen.
From Volume 2: *Zones of Pain*

IDÉA VILARIÑO

MAYBE THEN

Maybe if you saw Hiroshima
I mean Hiroshima *mon amour*
if you saw
if you spent two hours suffering like a dog
if you saw
how much it can hurt, burn
and twist the soul like that iron
strip away joy forever
like charred skin
and you saw that nevertheless
there are ways to go on living, staying around
bearing no visible wounds
I mean
then
maybe then you'd believe
maybe then you'd suffer
understand.

Translated by Louise B. Popkin.
From Volume 7: *These Are Not Sweet Girls*

Romelia Alarcón de Folgar

Irreverent Epistle to Jesus Christ

Christ,
come down from your cross and wash your hands.
wash your knees and your side,
comb your hair,
put on your sandals
and blend your footsteps
that are searching for you
on the mountain ranges and the sea,
over the land;
through the air,
along the wire fences of the roads.

You can solve anything,
everything's easy for you
and so . . .
what are you waiting for?
Why don't you come down from your cross right now?
Without parables, with bullets
and loose reefs sharp with vengeance
in your hands . . .

And let the towns be filled with freed men
and midday sun,
orchards, doves and roses
their petals still full bloom
and bugles that announce
peaceful mornings.
Christ,
come down from your cross
where thousands of men

hang crucified beside you:
wash your hands and their hands,
your knees and their knees,
your side and their sides;
wash your forehead and their foreheads
crowned with thorns.

Don't let your impassive martyrdom continue:
show your wrath,
come down from your cross,
mingle with the men who love you.

Translated by Alison Ridley.
From Volume 7: *These Are Not Sweet Girls*

Gabriela Mistral

The Useless Vigil

I forgot that your light foot
was transformed into ashes,
and, as during good times,
I ventured to find you
along the path.

I passed through valley,
plain and river;
songs filled me with melancholy.
Afternoon faded,
tumbled its luminous vase.
And you didn't appear!

The sun crumbled its poppy,
charred and lifeless.
A foggy fringe trembed
over the fields.
I was alone!

From a tree,
a whitened branch like an arm
rustled in the autumn wind.
I was terrified and cried out to you,
"My love, hurry to my side!"

I hold fear
and I hold on to love.
"My love, speed your journey!"
Night thickened around me;
my madness grew.

I forgot—they made you deaf
to my lament:
your deadly dawn,

your heavy hand,
too late, its quest for my hand,
and your wide eyes,
a sovereign inquisition!

Night extended
its bituminous-black pool.
The owl of mystic fortune
fretted the path
with the macabre silk
of its wings.
I will not call out to you again;
your journey has ended.
My naked foot continues its trek;
your foot remains eternally quiet.

In vain I hold this vigil
along deserted roads.
Your ghost will not come together
in my open arms!

Translated by Maria Giachetti.
From Volume 5: *A Gabriela Mistral Reader*

Marjorie Agosín

Disappeared Woman I

I am the disappeared woman,
in a country grown dark,
silenced by the
wrathful cubbyholes
of those with no memory.
You still don't see me?
You still don't hear me
in those peregrinations
through the dense smoke
of terror?
Look at me,
nights, days, soundless tomorrows
sing me
so that no one may
threaten me
call me
to give me back
name,
sounds,
a covering of skin
by naming me.

Don't conspire with
oblivion,
tear down the silence.
I want to be
the appeared woman
from among the labyrinths
come back, return
name myself.
Call my name.

Translated by Cola Franzen.
From Volume 2: *Zones of Pain*

Teresa Calderon

State of Siege

Considering the graveness
of the most recent events,
and the internal disorder
that is being lived in my country these days.
Considering also the continuous subversion of my sentiments
and the successive
insurrection
of my will,
I request reinforcements
from the Highest State of my conscience.

It emits an edict that
immediately establishes
the emergency situation,
and to protect the citizenry
it lines up a robust army
of defense mechanisms
with strict orders
to give up one's life if necessary.

My anarchic heart
accepts a provisional government,
while I continue
in clandestine negotiations with your eyes,
with your mouth invading all my limits,
in this war that you pronounce to me
in this open love between us.

DOMESTIC BATTLES

I began losing the battles.

Accordingly, I ended up losing you.

With a shadow radar
I pursue you among so many people.

There you are scrunched up in your trench
with an escort of accumulated hatred
unravelling kisses in a useless sheet.

With me you sustain the most savage struggle
because it is the last of all.

From now on I will be the guerilla fighter
the one who takes your mouth by storm
the one who installs her flag in your memory,

the one who dies of love in other arms
believing that she is invading
the distant territory of your body.

Translated by Celeste Kostopulos-Cooperman.
From Volume 7: *These Are Not Sweet Girls*

BELKIS CUZA MALÉ

WOMEN DON'T DIE ON THE FRONT LINES

Women Don't Die on the Front Lines
their heads don't roll like golf balls,
they don't sleep under a rain forest of gunpowder,
they don't leave the sky in ruins.
No snow freezes in their hearts.
Women don't die on the front lines,
they don't drive the devil out of Jerusalem
they don't blow up aqueducts or railroads,
they don't master the arts of war
or of peace, either.
They don't make generals
or unknown soldiers carved out of stone
in town squares.
Women don't die on the front lines.
They are statues of salt in the Louvre,
mothers like Phaedra,
lovers of Henry the Eighth,
Mata Haris,
Eva Perons,
queens counselled by prime ministers,
nursemaids, cooks, washerwomen,
romantic poets.
Women don't make history,
but at nine months they push it out of their bellies
then sleep for twenty-four hours
like a soldier on leave from the front.

Translated by Pamela Carmell.
From Volume 7: These Are Not Sweet Girls

ALAIDE FOPPA

WOUND

Your life hurts me, son,
like a recently opened wound.
They think that you have detached yourself from me
simply because you were born.
The cord is invisible:
an arrow in my side,
a ripened fruit
that does not abandon the tree,
a tender branch
threatened.
You are weaker than my hand,
more delicate than my eyes,
smoother than my lips.
You made me so vulnerable
that I feel fear:
your life depends on
a gust of wind,
whoever touches you lightly
hurts you,
at your side,
in the tepid folds
of your bed, death sleeps.
And even though you are
more mine than my hand,
oh my most tender little branch,
perhaps I won't know how to defend you.

Translated by Celeste Kostopulos-Cooperman.
From Volume 7: These Are Not Sweet Girls

BLANCA WIETHÜCHTER

WITHOUT HISTORIES

1.

We who are responsible for living
and have been born in the third world.

We who ask for justice
and live in South America.

We who die in Bolivia
disconsolate and alone

we are the history that cannot be written
and journey with the head cut off.

2.

A student is killed by a shot in the back.

The spilled blood
spreads over the street
like a cry.

Who could write about innocence?

Translated by Shaun T. Griffin and Emma Sepúlveda-Pulvirenti.
From Volume 7: These Are Not Sweet Girls

GIOCONDA BELLI

NICARAGUA WATER FIRE

Rain
Window view of water on leaves
wind passes swishing skirts
muddy waters uproot tree trunks
trees paint stars puddles of blood
borders of a day that must be fought
there's no other way no alternative but the struggle
Behind curtains of water
I write fingers on triggers
great wars
suffering the size of mothers' eyes
dripping uncontainable cloudbursts
here come the small cold corpses
los muchachos come down from the mountains
with hammocks they recovered from the Contras
we don't eat much there isn't much we all want to eat
big white hands want to kill us
but we made hospital beds
where women scream births
all day we beat like hearts
tum tum tum tum
Indians' veins repeat history:
We don't want children who will be slaves
flowers blossom from coffins
no one dies in Nicaragua
Nicaragua my love my raped child
getting up straightening her skirt
walking behind the murderer following him
down the mountain up the mountain
they will not pass say the birds
they will not pass say the couples who make love
who make children who make bread who make trenches
who make uniforms who write letters for the mobilized troops

Nicaragua my love my Black girl Miskito Sumo Rama
Maypole dance in Pearl lagoon
hurricane winds blowing down the San Juan River
they will not pass and it rains on the young soldiers
tracking the scent of the beasts
never letting them rest following them pursuing them
uprooting them from the motherland's breast ripping them
    out like weeds
never letting them strike
we want corn rice beans
seeds taking root in the land
where a *campesino* keeps his Land Reform title in a wooden box
don't let the devils pass to announce the coming salvation
to the people who saw farms burn
and a neighbor murdered in front of his wife and children
Nicaragua my child
she dances she's learned to read to talk with people
to tell them her story to get on planes to tell her story
to travel around the world telling her story to everyone
speaking tirelessly in newspapers written in incomprehensible
    languages
screaming getting angry furious
all the noise she makes seems incredible so does the way she resists
planes mines speedboats bombs curses in English
speeches on how to bow one's head
and she fights breaks free flees
and there goes General Sandino and the hill the rocket launchers
the green columns advancing clearing land
building sugar mills
rivers of milk houses schools
young men telling their story
limping from the hospital
taking a bus to return to the north
wind that shakes fear
we were born for this
we rejoice for this
rage and hope clenched between our teeth

no rest for us no rest for them day or night
tiny but stubborn country
Nicaragua fearless spear daring wild mare
pastures in Chontales where Nadine
dreams of Percheron horses
and we have a fountain of dreams
we have a factory of dreams
a dream assembly line for the unbelievers
here no one gets away without a scratched conscience
no one comes here without being moved
country of enlightened lunatics poets painters
showers of lights schools dance
international conferences protocol
school-age police sweetly scolding
flesh and blood of people who sometimes are right
     sometimes make mistakes
who try and try again
everything moves here a dancing woman's hips
singing out a lust for life against the mummies
speaking of death hoping to earn their return trips
on printed pages that come out in the afternoon with their lies
and their rage of frustrated hysteria
envy of the girl who sways as she walks
winks sells tamales sells nail polish
joins the militia goes to the park invents love
sets the flowers of the malinche tree on fire hides to bewilder
comes out marching amidst drawn bayonets
sets up the circus and fairs and prays
and believes in life and death
and prepares swords of fire
so that the only choice can be
earthly paradise
or else
patria libre
or *morir.*

Translated by Steven F. White.
From Volume 7: *These Are Not Sweet Girls*

ROSARIO AGUILAR

AN EXCERPT FROM
THE LOST CHRONICLES OF TERRA FIRMA

Doña Ana no longer wished to remain in Spain. She had already learned and seen enough. The cold climate, along with the dry, life-less landscape, saddened her. She wanted to return to her home and breathe once again its air.

One day she wrote the Queen for permission to return. She put the letter under her pillow for safekeeping. The Mother Superior found it there. No matter how much they asked Doña Ana about it, she would say nothing. She remained silent. If her confessor knew about it, he kept it a secret of confession....

> To Your Holy Roman Catholic Majesty,
> Empress and Our Lady the Queen:
>
> Doña Ana, the daughter of Taugema, chief of several of the tribes of the Province of Nicaragua, kisses the royal hands and feet of Your Majesty for the great favors you have conferred upon me, such as bringing me here to Spain to learn industrious trades. I have no doubt that Your Majesty is aware of my determination and heartfelt desire to return to my own land to marry and live the rest of my life there. A long time has passed since I wrote a letter to Your Majesty because I have felt so alone here in Spain. I am all alone. I came here a long time ago, and the boat that brought me here has since made many trips back and forth between Spain and my homeland. I am sad. Everything is sad here. I look out the window and in front of me I see arid, lifeless fields full of stones. The olive trees afflict me the most; they look like phantom

trees. They are nothing like our real trees. And how cold
it is here! I will never get used to this cold climate. I wrap
myself in blankets and wear woolen socks, yet I am still
cold. I long for the warmth of my homeland. I am isolat-
ed and feel a great emptiness. In the convent they look at
me and treat me like some strange, rare being. The nuns
don't trust me. I'm desperate, really desperate! I don't
want to die here: my death recorded in the King's books,
"She died of homesickness and sadness." I need to
breathe the air of my homeland. I can't stand being
closed up in the convents and houses here. There, in
Nicaragua, we live with our doors and windows open.
The air passes from one end of the house to the other.
No one opens or locks a door to enter or leave.

It saddens me to depart without seeing you. I so much
wanted to meet you. I want to leave you my memoirs,
writings from the time I was a child when they taught me
how to write Castilian correctly. This way, you can learn
some of the details.

When I was a child we lived joyfully. I was the daugh-
ter of an important family, that of a chieftain.
Everything was happiness and celebrations. We lived life
with great joy. We had our songs. The green fields of
maize. We played in the squares and bathed in the rivers.
We would go to the markets where every kind of fruit
could be found: *pitahayas rojas, nísperos, caimitos, zapotes,
mameyes*, tomatoes...and my favorite, *jocotes*. Wasps, spar-
rows, and hummingbirds flew about. In our feasts we
drank *chicha* made of fermented maize or the sap of the
coyol palm and cacao drink. Everything was abundant.
Life was peaceful and simple. One day, all of the women
from the prominent families went to bathe in the river.
We were in the water, playing, splashing around...when
suddenly it sounded to us as if the earth were beating like
a drum. We looked around in all directions. We stopped
what we were doing; we stopped singing our song. We

were silent. Someone put an ear to the ground to detect whether it was an earthquake, a volcano, or a flock of animals. A threat, a misfortune. Oh! When the first animal appeared it was so horrible that we thought it was a ghost. It had two heads: one of them like the head of a deer, but with long hair; the other was like a white-faced, bearded monkey. They had six feet: four of them with hooves, and two that hung down from above. Then, more and more of these animals appeared. We were frightened and terribly astonished. Although we were naked, we took off running for the bushes to hide ourselves. There was not enough time to pick up any of our things...our skirts were left strewn about.... There, behind some bushes in the mud, we kept silent; without moving we observed them. We saw, heard, and smelled them. When they went away—after drinking some water—we ran to our village. We arrived, all of us shouting together at the same time: "You should have seen, you should have seen what we just saw." But the men did not believe us until they saw them with their own eyes.

Everything was happiness until the day that the Christians arrived. The water of the rivers flowed freely and cleanly. The fields yielded their ears of maize, the cacao trees, their beans. The joyous men would get drunk in their celebrations, the women gave birth to their children, the animals mated and grew fat....

At first they wanted peace, so they could teach us about their god. Later, baptizing everyone was not enough. They wanted our land and sought to enslave us to work in their mines and fields.

We couldn't live. Our hearts froze. All our songs grew mute in our throats.... We tried to carry on in spite of them: milling maize with the grindstone, preparing the dough, tossing the tortillas on the stoves of three stones. May their weapons of war not kill us, may they permit us to pray to our gods, may they let us live.... We just want to live.

I so wanted to meet you, beloved Empress, Queen, Our Lady. I am Doña Ana the Indian, daughter of Chief Taugema. In my land we only wish to live in peace. In the past, our ancestors also had to flee from ambitious, warlike men.

I want to tell you that before the Spaniards arrived, we had the most cultivated and populated lands. Everything was organized. Our men had specific seasons for planting, for prayer, for abstaining from their women, for fasting, and for dancing and getting drunk. The women had times for weaving, for going to market, for grinding, for lying down with males, for giving birth, and raising children. Everything was foreseen: the summer months, the rainy season, the windy season; everything, that is, except the untimely and violent arrival of the foreigners. We like your god because he stands for love and forgiveness, and we cherish love. We like his virgin mother because she knows how to console under her protective shawl. We accept your religion, especially the part that goes "Love god above all things, love your neighbor as you love yourself, sanctify your feast days, honor your elders." We like that. That is very fine. It seems to us that our gods and your merciful god and his beloved mother—so pretty and good—could live together in heaven. It appears to us that those under your orders preach all the beautiful things about your religion but do not practice them.... At times they are so cruel and violent!

Everything became complicated, dear Queen. Neither of us will ever be the same, neither your people nor ours, nor shall we ever live the same way again, ever. If your people were to leave now, nothing could be as it was before. How is it possible to retrace one's footsteps, to ignore that which is known, to separate that which has been united, or purify that which has already been mixed? It would be nice if you could leave us your god and his

mother! Leave them with us, don't take them away from
us on your ships.... If I could just go to the Royal
Chambers and speak with Your Majesties face to face, kiss
your hands and feet. If you would allow me to travel to
Rome and speak with His Holiness! Because there must
be reform of the laws and the religion that you have taught
us.

She who kisses your royal hands and feet,
Doña Ana the Indian
(signature and seal)

Translated by Edward Waters Hood.
From Volume 10: *The Lost Chronicles of Terra Firma*

CARMEN NARANJO

THE COMPULSIVE COUPLE
OF THE HOUSE ON THE HILL

When they met, he set out the conditions explicitly. Marriage is a
serious commitment, especially when you're ambitious and power-hun-
gry; besides, you're already accustomed to a certain lifestyle and aren't
looking for change, and as if that were not enough, marriage is a tricky
business because when it is a question of catching the fish, everything
is just fine, and only afterwards come the complaints, protests, grudges
and infinite bitching.

The day was dark and it was barely two o'clock in the afternoon.
The dense air hung heavily, in spite of the open windows and the rau-
cous fan that snored with the rhythm of dry heaves. He was sweating
moderately; she profusely, flushed with the heat and the anguish that
was written all over her face. I'm not one of those women who's fick-
le and I love you and I will always love you just the same. My only con-
cern will be to please you, to please you in every way, even when I
don't know how, I will never complain, never. You wouldn't mistrust
me if you knew me better.

Outside, the noisy birds were lamenting the rain and it wasn't even
raining that day. It rained for the wedding, a year and a half later. She
arrived first, with only the relatives that he had invited because he didn't
think all of them were suitable. Not her carpenter uncle and his family
because they were gluttons and stupid; not her cousins from that
detestable dusty town because they were ignorant and they embraced
you too enthusiastically and anyway they smelled of bologna; not her
brothers-in-law because they were ugly and because the way they
laughed betrayed their imbecility.

She arrived, serene and pale. No one noticed the slight trembling of
her left hand. Her white, chiseled face would have revealed even to the

164

casual observer a year and a half of confinement, a year and a half of complying with instructions that were increasingly stringent, increasingly severe, a year and a half of silence because she had learned to say only what he wanted to hear, a year and a half without girlfriends, whom she was losing one by one because you give your heart to me completely, leaving no room for anyone else and from now on I am your father, your mother and your whole life.

He arrived half an hour later, the impertinent rain and his torn pants having kept him, not to mention the folly of so many people participating in an act as stupid as a wedding.

The ceremony was longer than it had to be and uncomfortable—he grunted several times and tapped his foot repeatedly, as if he thought it necessary to retort: pure foolishness this stuff the priest is saying because he doesn't even know what the matrimonial yoke is.

When they left, after the rain had slackened to an inoffensive drizzle, he elbowed her to look at the hill: there we will have a house up high, and when I'm mayor I'll wave to the people from the balcony. She said that yes, it would be a lovely house, and that she was already dreaming about caring for it meticulously so that he would be happy and feel utterly proud. He replied that everything would be his decision and done to suit his tastes.

It is said that they were deeply happy. He always walked in front of her on their walks from exactly six-thirty until seven-forty-five on the dot. Precisely two steps in front. Each night she seemed a little smaller, as if she were shrinking. Perhaps it was a simple optical illusion; perhaps it was the hunched-over posture with which she combined her short steps.

They built their house high on top of the hill. White with a red roof. The balcony presided over a simple architecture of symmetrical windows and, perpendicular to the balcony, a narrow door with a bronze door-knocker.

Things went well for them in their business dealings. He had an instinct for opportunity and prices; she was thrifty, with a passion for effficiency, constant work and taking advantage of things that on the surface seemed useless. Their assets grew with the purchase of a supermarket, then a bookstore with a little printing press in the rear and finally a hardware store with a repair shop for those machines now known as appliances.

Of course they did have problems managing their employees. He dictated a moral and behavioral code, replete with duties and the most explicit details of how and when, which categorically prohibited them from taking liberties with anything regarding the business accounts, with anyone else's affairs, with punctuality and with absences. The mere idea of getting sick was out of the question, not to mention coming to work sick (fear of contagion). She was an all-vigilant eye for absolute compliance to what was in the code. The first employees ended up leaving but then acquired such a reputation for being bad workers that they couldn't find other jobs, and they went far away, where their infamy hadn't reached. The other employees stayed for years, more out of fear of exile than anything else, since besides the nuisance of having to work constantly and to practice excessive courtesy, the salary wasn't incentive enough anyway and a good part of what there was went to the necessities of ties and coats, and to being clean shaven with a military cut (straight up and well scraped).

Their only son was born after five years of marriage, when gossip was already rampant that the poor woman was sterile; so thin, pale, shrunken and, besides, the couple probably went to bed the same distance apart as on their routine walks, in silence, from exactly six-thirty to seven-forty-five on the dot. The pregnancy wasn't obvious because she used to wear an ample housecoat, which kept those tongues of verbal journalism wagging in parlors, in markets and in formal and informal encounters, about whether she was really pregnant or if the baby was adopted. The doubt remained for a long time, as we will see later on.

In the main inventory ledger, he wrote in an accountant's calligraphy: male, seven and a half pounds, fifty-two centimeters long, ugly, and a crier. After two days she went back to work, a little paler and bent over a little more, wearing a proud smile but paying no attention to the congratulations offered her, and she never even acknowledged the little presents the employees brought her. Enough already, he had said about them sticking their noses into places they didn't belong.

He tried to become mayor by the traditional means: courting the politicians from this party and that (since one must be prudent), and throwing banquets for them and giving them modest contributions (since there were diminishing returns). And then nothing. After their victories, they couldn't recall having met him.

The flood that year from the torrential, endless rains, which didn't stop even in time to dry out the balcony that had been converted into a shimmering pool where crickets and fallen leaves splashed, brought him his long-awaited opportunity. The rising waters from the two streams, inoffensive in the summer, swept away entire neighborhoods of houses made of mud, tin, cardboard, old rags and rotten wood. Thousands were left hungry and homeless. Two old women and seven children who were sleeping in hammocks were found, bloated, among the rocks when the waters receded.

He raised the prices in his chain of businesses but invented opportune charity. In the supermarket, long lines formed for the handout of a hard roll. In the hardware store one could get a burlap shirt. In the bookstore the free item was the prayer, "Lord deliver us from our sins."

With a dictionary and the patience to carefully scour twenty pages a day, he found the word that described him: philanthropist: "he who professes love for his peers and tries to improve their lot in life." He demanded that it precede his name each time someone addressed him. She was the first to call him Mister Philanthropist and at work it soon spread. The majority of their customers, not knowing the meaning of the word, believed he had changed his name, and without much difficulty they began to call him "don Philanthropist."

And the title was being reinforced with small acts: whatever was truly useless from the inventory was to be donated to the hospital, to the school, to the community center; the wilted vegetables wouldn't be sold for a few cents to don Anibal's pig farm; repackaged, they could be distributed to the poor on Saturdays at two o'clock on the dot; and, with the paper that yellowed, he decided to produce bimonthly almanacs to give to his customers, with the holidays and the lunar movements as well as blurbs of propaganda for his businesses, in which it was always mentioned that his principal concern was purely philanthropical.

The politicians visited him again, this time not to ask for a contribution, but to offer him the post of mayor. After they had nominated him the first time, reelections followed until what had to happen happened.

One of his first acts was to set aside the date of January second of each year for receiving the public from the balcony of his house high on top of the hill. He, above, would list an inventory of all he had accomplished, mixing some thoughts about moral and practical order in with the details. She, below, standing in the doorway that opened to the kitchen, would pass out corn liquor in paper cups and some homemade cookies. Then they would turn up the radio, tuned to the station that broadcast whatever music was popular, and some young and rhythmic couples would try out their moves on the pavement.

Yes, that tradition of the second of January lasted for a long time, but one day it ended.

Their son was growing and he wasn't dark like his father, nor long of face like his mother, but he was troublesome like both. He began with tantrums, which neither punishment nor reward could stop. They tried beating him; it was useless. They offered him more expensive gifts, if only he would stop shouting and kicking for a while, but to no avail. They finally gave up and let him do whatever he felt like and then he began to spit at mealtime and to break valuable objects and to mock his parents in the most ridiculous ways he could. They tied him up in a dark room but he managed to escape; they would hide him when visitors arrived but he would appear at the most interesting part of the conversation to pee in the center of the rug. They didn't know what to do. He said the boy was like his mother and she, while never directly contradicting him, would answer that she couldn't recall ever behaving like that. Finally, they decided that the best solution would be to send him to one of those correctional centers, to see if they could work a miracle.

They didn't see him for many years, not even during vacations, or at Christmas, or on anniversaries or birthdays. Nevertheless, in truth his absence weighed on them, as did the recurring nightmare that he would return unchanged. They sent the monthly check on time, but they never opened any correspondence that came from the institution, so they knew nothing of his progress or his setbacks. Then the day arrived that both had awaited with an intemperate fear that kept them awake at nights: the refund that the director brought them, in person—along with a bill for five zeros preceded by a seven—because that scowling young man with the aggressive stare, a lascivious beginning of a mustache, long, curly hair, that thin, tall young man with his shoulders thrown back as if he expected a punch or were about to throw one, had burned down an entire building at the institution. He didn't smile nor say how do you do and entered like a dog with its tail between its legs. They wrote out the check and, excusing themselves without waiting to hear anything more, bid farewell to the director. They offered him neither a seat nor a glass of water even though the day was hot, a day with a brilliant, intruding sun that caused migraines with its harsh reflections in shoe buckles, in tooth fillings and in everything that shimmered.

From then on they never spoke with their son. He did whatever he took a fancy to, getting up much later than his parents, eating some fruit, and then on a whim that changed with the rhythm of the music, turning up the radio to its maximum volume, until the shrill tones seemed about to explode. When his parents came in, he would begin to sing, in a soft voice, the most shameless of mambos, cumbias and meringues, and then he would leave to roam the streets at all hours of the night until a fuzzy pre-dawn made ghosts of the bushes and the huts that had begun to burgeon again near the streams.

The mayor blessed the days that were calm; his wife made promises while she prayed novena after novena amidst the sums of the invoices, the list of orders and her responsibilities to the customers.

But the complaints began to arrive. At first they were timid. Don Anibal, rubbing his hands with the air of a diplomat beginning the process of an appeal, spoke of two dead pigs—his best purebred ones and already sold at a very good price—that the boy killed with arrows the night before last when the moon shone like a breast full of milk. They took care of it with a check and a plea for his silence. The list continued, ranging from a broken window to a rape in the park, right there in the corner of the lilies that were ruined worse than the poor girl, the illegitimate daughter—it was said—of Pascual the drayman and who knows for sure who her mother was but she appeared in the arms of the crippled Chepa, who shouted "She's a gift from God!"

One night, almost in the shadow of the doorway, at seven-forty-five on the dot, he walked back two steps and shouted at her: "It's over. I'm going to kill him!" She, as if expecting that and worse, answered in an unswerving voice, "Your will be done." They didn't go to bed, sitting instead in uncomfortable chairs in the foyer, where they used to receive those bothersome men who brought them complaints about pipes and sewers, and waited until midnight. When they were nodding off, their mouths open, the slamming of the door aroused them. "Mother, Father," said the youth, kneeling before them, "I'm going to change, I want to be a useful man, a revolutionary." They couldn't budge. They really didn't believe him; they were the kind of people that prayed for miracles without faith.

But the change did take place; the boy entered school, serious, with books under his arm that he actually read and studied, he got wonderful grades, associated with the best people, even went to the most humble ghettos where he taught the poor to read and add and subtract. Educated, sober, he spoke very little with his parents, just whatever was necessary. Of course he never followed the strict code demanded by family life, and on one memorable occasion he even said to a servant in that loud voice meant for everyone to hear, "Those pricks are two petty, compulsive, heartless imbeciles." That hurt them slightly; it wasn't enough to offend them nor to brood over. The change had been that miraculous.

He continued suspecting, she continued with her promises and novenas of gratitude, but deep down they couldn't understand the change and for a long time they rather expected a knife in the back.

The son went to the capital, to go to college. They breathed more easily, since at least they would have a long rest and perhaps luck would have it that he wouldn't find his way back home because it's pretty there—city lights, all kinds of entertainment and girls who know how to stimulate the mind, although perhaps there wasn't much there to stimulate.

The second of January was celebrated from then on with more splendor, since they needed to replenish lost prestige and make everyone forget the many years they had been corrupting the office and tiring the public, lest anyone begin to think that a new broom might sweep better than the old one. They served beer instead of corn liquor and bologna sandwiches instead of cookies. One January second the mayor, after exaggerating the feats of his government and citing as his own some things that had been done by international organizations and volunteer associations, meditated out loud (so he said) about human ingratitude, even that of one's own children, and pointed out that philanthropy doesn't always reap gratitude. As his voice was trembling, he stirred emotion in some, especially when they saw his wife handing out the beers with eyes that welled up as if they were about to flood. They didn't know that the poor thing was suffering from a crippling flu that had arrived from the port in the form of an epidemic.

The son returned home, without the girl who stimulates minds. He didn't even let his parents know, nor did he visit them. He set up a law practice in a poor neighborhood and lived in the back room. A good litigator, he won hopeless cases, in eternal disputes over water rights and farm boundaries, and thus his reputation spread and people from all over, even from the capital, consulted him. He dressed cleanly and simply, and the depth of his eyes was striking. A pretty little husband-hunter noted that his look was messianic. Although few understood the term, many repeated it because it sounded nice.

When it came time for the election, he ran for mayor. That really shook up the people: father against son. Then the speeches began and what a way of speaking the boy had, clear and peremptory, concrete and sincere, especially when he talked about eradicating philanthropy so that truth and justice could thrive; and ending all these monopolies, the hardware store, the printing press, bookstore and supermarket, all with high prices and terrible products, so that people could establish honorable, free businesses; he ridiculed the compulsive little habits of that compulsive couple of the house high on top of the hill.

He won the election by such an absolute majority that according to his own count, the old mayor received votes from only himself, his wife, two servants and five of his employees. Devastated, they took a vacation to the coast, not even waiting until the inauguration. Their first vacation in twenty-seven years of marriage, and they didn't know what resting was all about nor what one could do if one didn't work. The truth was that their only wish was to go to the sea and cry and cry. Both had the idea that it was easier and more comfortable to cry by the ocean.

The young mayor arrived for his first day of work exactly on time. In his hand he was carrying his first memo: "I categorically prohibit anyone from speaking to me from behind because that always gives me a chill; anyone who shakes hands with me must first wash his hands, I'm allergic to dust and dirt; I don't want anyone to rearrange my papers and please no smoking in my presence, the odor of tobacco makes me nauseous; someone less importent should take care of small nuisances, as only the most important matters should come to my attention, those things that require a difficult and intelligent solution; upon my entrance one should say to me simply, "Good day, Mr. Mayor," on my exit, "Good night, Mr. Mayor." As soon as we're better acquainted, I will give you further instructions."

And that is just how it happened. And that and other matters which don't fit into this story, like the conditions that he expressed very clearly and categorically to the young woman to whom he raised the possibility of marriage, confirmed in the town that he really was, after all, the legitimate son of the compulsive couple of the house high on the hill.

Translated by Linda Britt.
From Volume 3: Landscapes of a New Land

CLEMENTINA SUÁREZ

POEM FOR MANKIND AND ITS HOPE

I look now within myself
and am so distant,
budding in hidden spaces,
rootless, no tears, no crying out.
—Complete within myself—
in my own hands,
in the world of tenderness
created by my own flesh.

I have watched myself be born, grow, without a sound,
without branches of aching arms,
subtle, silent, with no words to wound,
nor womb overflowing with fish.

Like a dream-rose my world was fashioned,
Angels of love were always faithful to me
in the poppy, in joy and blood.

Every seashell traced my path
and taught me the moment to arrive.
And I learned to be on time
For my date with water, ash
and despair...

Fragile was my tree, but always vibrant
To man and bird I have been constant,
I have loved as the geraniums must,
like children, like the blind.

But on any scale
I was always out of bounds,

because my impeccable and recently new world
chews up old facades,
fashions and useless habits.

My caress is combat
urgency to live,
prophecy of a demanding sky
that footsteps outside sustain.

I create the eternal,
within and without me,
in search of my universe.
I learned, arrived, entered,
with full knowledge
that the poet who walks alone
is like a dead man, an exile,
an Archangel who kneels to hide his face,
a hand that drops its star
and denies himself and his people
their acquired or supposed inheritance.

From this blind and absurd death or life,
my world was born,
my poem and my name.
This is why I speak tirelessly of man,
of man and his hope.

Translated by Janet N. Gold.
From Volume 7: These Are Not Sweet Girls

SECTION IV
WOMEN AND LANGUAGE

LUISA VALENZUELA

DIRTY WORDS

Good girls can't say these things, neither can elegant ladies nor any other women. They can't say these things or other things, for there is no possibility of reaching the positive without its opposite, the exposing and exposed negative. Not even the other women, the ones who aren't so lady-like, can utter these words categorized as "dirty." The big ones, the fat ones: *swearwords*. These words that are so delicious to the palate, that fill the mouth. *Swearwords*. These words that completely spare us from the horror gathered in a brain almost ready to explode. There are cathartic words, moments of speech that should be inalienable and that have been alienated from us since time immemorial.

During childhood, mothers or fathers—why always blame women—washed our mouths with soap and water when we said some of these so-called swearwords, "dirty" words, when we expressed our truth. Then came better times, but those unloving interjections and appellatives remained forever dissolved in detergent soapsuds. To clean, to purify the word, the best possible form of repression. This was known in the Middle Ages, and in the darkest regions of Brittany, France, until recently. Witches' mouths—and we are all witches today—are washed with red salt to purify them. Substituting one orifice for the other, as Margo Glantz would say, the mouth was and continues to be the most threatening opening of the feminine body: it can eventually express what shouldn't be expressed, reveal the hidden desire, unleash the menacing differences which upset the core of the phallogocentric, paternalistic discourse.

No sooner said than done, from the spoken word to the written word: just one step. Which requires all the courage we can muster because we believe that it is so simple; however, it isn't because writing will overcome all the abysses and so one must have an awareness of the initial danger, of the abyss. We must forget the washed mouths, allow the mouths to bleed till we gain access to the territory in which everything can and should be said. Knowing that there is so much to explore, so many barriers yet to be broken through.

It is a slow and untiring task of appropriation. A transformation of that language consisting of "dirty" words that were forbidden to us for centuries, and of the daily language that we should handle very carefully, with respect and fascination because in some way it doesn't belong to us. We are now tearing down and rebuilding; it is an arduous task. Dirtying those washed mouths, taking possession of the punishment, with no room for self-pity.

Among us, crying is prohibited. Other emotional manifestations, other emotions no, but crying yes, prohibited. We can, for example, give estrus free reign and be happy. Jealousy, on the other hand, we must maintain under strict control; it could degenerate into weeping.

Why so much fear of tears? Because the masks we use are made of salt. A stinging, red salt which makes us beautiful and majestic but devours our skin.

Beneath the red masks, our faces are raw and the tears could well dissolve the salt and uncover our sores. The worst penitence.

We cover ourselves with salt and the salt erodes us and protects us at the same time. Red salt, the most beautiful of all and the most destructive. Long ago, they scrubbed our mouths with the red salt of infamy and we remained branded forever. Witches, they accused us, they persecuted us, until we learned how to take possession of that salt and we made beautiful masks for ourselves. Iridescent, skin-toned, translucent with promise.

Now if they want to kiss us—and sometimes they still do— they have to kiss the salt and burn their lips. We know how to respond to kisses and we don't mind being burnt with them from the other side of the mask. They/us, us/they. The salt now joins us, the sores join us and only weeping can bring us apart.

We mate with our masks on, and sometimes the thirsty come to lick us. It is a perverse pleasure: they become more

> thirsty than ever and it hurts and the dissolution of the
> masks terrifies us. They lick more and more, they moan in
> desperation, we moan with pain and fear. What will
> become of us when our stinging faces outcrop? Who will
> want us without a mask, in raw flesh?
> They won't. They will hate us for that, for having licked
> us, for having exposed us. And we wouldn't have even shed
> a tear nor allowed ourselves our most intimate gesture: the
> self-disintegration of our mask thanks to the prohibited
> weeping that opens furrows in order to begin again.

Now our mask is the text, the one that we ourselves, the women,
the keepers of textuality and texture, can dissolve if we care to—or not.
Reconstruct it, modify it, make our own those words that for others
were dirty—dirty in our female mouths, of course—and use that which
was meant to stigmatize us in order to arm, as always, our defensive
shells. Between two hard covers. Reflect our images in the book, in
the text, the other face of the female body, even though it may not be
conspicuously female, even though it may elicit the doubtful compli-
ment that we have all probably heard at one time.

"But what an excellent novel (or short story, or poem): it seems like
a man's writing!"

At one time, perhaps, we would have been flattered by such non-
sense. Now we know. It seems, but it is not. Because what we have ulti-
mately come to learn best is to read, to read and decipher according to
our own codes.

For a long time now we have been writing bit by bit, each time more
fiercely and with greater self-awareness. Women in the arduous task of
constructing with materials inscribed by the other. Constructing not
from zero, which would have been easier, but rather transgressing the
barriers of censorship, destroying the canons in search of that authen-
tic voice which can't be destroyed by anything, not soap nor rock salt,
not the fear of castration, nor tears.

Translated by Cynthia Ventura.
From Volume 6: Pleasure in the Word

ANGELA HERNÁNDEZ

HOW TO GATHER
THE SHADOWS OF THE FLOWERS

"Voyage of voyages with a hundred returns / capricious voyages / testimony of sighs / returns without turns / time in bouquets / and in my brow a sacred zeal to fade away / perhaps to return."

We found this text under the mattress and, like the rest of them, it seemed intended to provide us with clues to understand her. An impossible enterprise for us who had known her and loved her as a common girl, as the eldest sister, for whom our parents reserved certain privileges.

Faride was the only one of us to attend a private school (Papa got her a scholarship to an Evangelical institute). The rest of us went to public school. When she finished high school, she started working as a cashier in a supermarket; she remained in that job for six months. One day, surprisingly, she quit. Mama accused her of acting unconscionably, a judgment ratified by my father's recriminating glances. They both employed every possible means to extract from her the reason for her self-dismissal. She had not been laid off, nor had she had any difficulties in balancing the register every day, nor any trouble with any customer. It was not until after many weeks of siege that she said: "The supervisor kept pawing me." Nobody bothered her about it again. Two months later she began to work in a fabric shop. That's how she was, unaffected, serious, and reserved. I have brought you some photographs, but I must return them right away. My mother has forbidden us to touch her belongings.

From the very first glance the photographs captured my attention; I was intrigued above all by the well-defined combination of white and black features in one face: thick lips, very fine nose, long and kinky curls. In her eyes you caught a glimpse of an expression as dual and marked as the lines of her profile; there was in them a latent force: a vague expressiveness, a black blaze behind a deceiving curtain of void. From that day on, the image of her

*seductive gaze has been an obsessive burden in my brain. After that I would
stay with José after class to hear more details.*

The women of my family marry before they turn twenty. My grand-
mother married very young; my mother followed the tradition, and
Faride got married a few months before turning eighteen. I don't
think she had a good idea of what marriage meant; I'm not even sure
whether she was happy or not, but I do remember her clearly, dis-
tressed and nervous, untiringly knitting tablecloths and bedcovers the
year before Raúl left for the United States. Not that she had much
choice. Faride supported the household. They had two children and
had been married four years and he still had not found a steady job.
When she returned to our house with the children, she seemed sad
and somewhat relieved.

*I have turned this information over and over in my mind, trying to under-
stand the meaning of the events that took place in José's house. I haven't
found anything that points to Faride having been subject to any special cir-
cumstances in her childhood and adolescence. There were nine siblings, who
received the same upbringing and grew up in the same house. Three of them,
including Faride, were born in the central mountains, but that doesn't make
them different. The two eldest brothers seem to have nothing in common
with her; José, the sixth child, whom I know best, is as normal a young man
as they come.*

Industrious and conscientious, when she moved back into the
house Faride continued working in the shop and knitting tablecloths
and bedcovers in the evenings and weekends. Her friends would say
to her jokingly: "Aha! knitting while she awaits her husband, like
Penelope," and she would reply with a smile: "I knit to eat, not to
deceive myself."

In some ways, in some small things, my sister's behavior was dif-
ferent from that of other people. She showed no special interest in her
physical appearance. She never wore lipstick or eye makeup. Her
wardrobe was very simple; she made her own clothes of light fabrics
and pastel colors; lemon yellow and lilac predominated in her apparel.
I was the oldest of the siblings still living at home; I was then just past
twelve; I don't remember ever seeing her angry at me; she never lec-
tured me, nor did she offer advice on any subject. But these details of

behavior don't make anyone special; least of all in our house, where chattering and long conversations between adults were extremely rare and where everyone preferred to keep to themselves; my mother listened to the radio; my father played dominoes; my older brothers cruised the streets; Faride knitted.

We got along very well with her and the children; life followed its natural course and none of us, not even our parents, had noticed the gradual transformation taking place within our sister; it was with great surprise that we witnessed the unexpected eruption of the world brewing within her. It happened at breakfast:

"He'll help me, this one will indeed help me, Mama. This man is really worth it. He is beautiful like a sun. He smells of May, he tastes like mint washed by a rain shower. He's not rich, nor young; he's not even heroic. But he's incomparably loving. He carries me to bed every day, and you should see what a bed, soft like a song filtered through water. He only needs a glance to understand me; he knows what I yearn for just from sensing it."

We couldn't quite understand her words. Not even Papa and Mama seemed to understand, since they were looking at her with puzzled expressions on their faces.

"The house has burst into flower in the few days we have spent together. Flowers assumed gigantic proportions with every minute of love. Violets and poppies growing deliriously; fennel and sunflowers and red wine-colored hollyhocks like open umbrellas. It's like a jungle now. The orchids climb the walls, forming very elegant nosegays, they barely let you see anything through the glass. The whole house is made of transparent glass. At first I was embarrassed; someone could see us when we did things in bed. Then I realized that the house was alone in the world. Swarms of bees embroider honey hives around the stalks of the carnations, green crickets and fireflies gather pollen to build their homes. Ah, the hollyhocks fascinate me with the red wine blood exquisitely retained in their corollas! Please advise me: What can one do with a garden gone out of control? What would we do if the flowers continue to climb to the ceiling and manage to conceal the sun? He could abandon me. He knows the garden grows only for me. What tragic pleasure! What sweet mortification!"

We remained silent. We couldn't understand her speech, but it fascinated us; Mama and Papa looked at her in astonishment. She got up, washed her hands, took her purse, and left.

The children delighted in our daughter's stories as if they were fairy tales. We got very agitated; we had never heard Faride talk about men, least of all in such insolent terms. We went over the details of the past week, and not finding anything extraordinary to justify her words, we decided to question her when she returned.

She didn't come back until eight o'clock that night and didn't even allow us to approach her: "I'm dying to sleep," she said as she threw herself onto the bed between her children without changing clothes. She was snubbing us for the first time in her life, and the disrespect of her action poisoned our evening.

The correspondences between their description of Faride's words and her writings were remarkable. The papers she left in her own handwriting share a similar tone. In one and the other the central mystery derives from the comparison between her discourse and her slight intellectual training. Where did these figurations come from? Was it perhaps a peculiar type of schizophrenia? Sometimes her brother worries me; more than by vocation, he has chosen this career with the hope of solving her enigma, and perhaps he's only moving further and further away from the clues.

We had been watching for her when she came in and sat next to me at the table. She seemed peaceful, cheerful; there was a disconcerting clarity in her eyes; two drops of dew hung from her pupils. A serenity and happiness which I felt spreading through my body.

I shuddered, my hands shook, when I saw her approach. A presentiment oppressed my heart. I saw the six-year-old girl with a wide ribbon holding her hair, the lively girl who grabbed my legs and whom I pushed away with a slap; the angel of light who kissed me, licked my lips, hugged me, caressed my breasts, and whom I pushed away, annoyed because two younger children demanded my attention; the insistent girl that got under my skirt wanting to play, and whom I spanked because I had too much work and her moving bothered me; the little one who at dawn cuddled at my feet hoping to remain unnoticed, and whom I would put back to bed screaming at her to be quiet. The one who would take care of her little brothers and sisters so I would love her more, the one who asked me to let her suckle when I breast-fed her little brother, the one who exasperated me with her cajoling, when it was already too late. The same face, the same ribbon, the same laugh, the same eyes. I would have wanted to hug her, but too much time and distance had passed between the two of us.

"I gave him a shell of twelve colors. Uf! it was so hard to find. It was between rocks, in a big hollow. I placed a strong tree trunk across the hollow, hung from it and walked with my hands to where the treasure was. It is the size of a teacup. The colors spring from the outside and then spread to the inside. It is so curious, so many colors emerging from a dark little knot."

She lowered her voice, as if she were speaking to herself; then she continued, excitedly. "He loved my gift. C'est très joli, comme la vie, he said to me."

My mother contained herself. Who is he? she asked her. Faride looked at her, puzzled, and replied naturally: "The director of the Oncology Institute.

"I never imagined he would be so beautiful. When he laughs, and he's almost always laughing, he leans back, chair and all. His laughter soars to the sky like bubbles of music coming out of a flute. I feel like sucking his mouth, I feel like eating him with lettuce and carnations. His teeth look moist. His laughter flows from inside, as if a glass of water flowered in his throat."

Mama blushed; Papa was uncomfortable in his chair; we were enjoying the story.

"He has requested me as his assistant in his operations, in the radioactive treatments and the laboratory. I tell him I know nothing of diseases and healing. He soothes me with his beautiful laughter; you'll learn, we'll teach you. We spent long dead hours, no, better still, living, gloriously living hours seated in two wooden chairs, on the rocks, by the sea. The others were far away. The rocks jutted out of the sea, we sailed on an indigo air several meters above the water."

Then, deep in thought, she commented to herself, "This special man makes me forget cancer." She devoured her breakfast and left hurriedly. We remained there talking about cancer. For some of us it was a bumblebee with horns, to others a plant with white spots. Unable to agree, we asked Mama. Anguished, she replied: "It's many things at the same time."

My husband and I were troubled. We had educated Faride as a good Christian and didn't recognize her in these daring speeches. We even came to suspect that she was keeping bad company, but anyway, people don't change just like that, from one moment to the next.

"They're dreams. Did you notice today? They're only dreams."

"She believes they're real. This is very unusual. She'll go telling those filthy stories around. They'll say she's a tramp. The husband working in New York and she living with other men."

"People who know us won't take her words seriously."

On Monday Mama woke us up early; she made us have breakfast and get ready for school in a hurry. Before we left, however, she couldn't prevent our overhearing our sister telling her in the kitchen:

"Mama, the young ones are darlings. His name is Andrés and Lucía introduced me to him at her party. Fire at first sight! One look and we were captivated. It's understandable: tender, passionate, soft, with his big green eyes, he's like a big son between my legs."

I found the piece of paper on the nightstand in her room; it was in her handwriting, and the contents seemed to refer to the story of the shell and the doctor. I woke her up very early, dawn had not yet broken. I took her to the kitchen, I wanted to speak to her without interruptions. Maybe the paper would clarify something, maybe her stories were nothing more than ideas copied from some disturbing book. "What is this? I asked her.

"Can't you see? I wrote it night before last: I am a relative of the stones / of the delicate waves of the coast / of the fragile horizons / the ever winding and unwinding snails / rocking in the vigils of their chiaroscuro moves / with their easy melodies / with their sonority of distant sea / with their peaceful and oblivious song / with mother-of-pearl winding and unwinding around submarine lines / drinking them like wine, like salt, like elementary milk."

She had repeated from memory the words on the piece of paper; she half-closed her eyes and continued to recite, as if she were reading something written inside her lids:

"Wet and surprised / like a newborn / I can barely touch myself /

I did not take the sun, there was no time / nor did I learn my tongue / nor did I detect the clues to my surroundings / I lie on myself / drowsy and timid / my textures are tender / in this my very embryo / sometimes I renew myself."

I felt a tingle down my spine. I didn't dare interrupt her, it wasn't my daughter talking.

"To exist and not to be / is a miracle / to be the frontier to the undecipherable / equidistant to acceptance / a wisdom on the margin of precepts / a lucid candor / a hidden golden vertebra / a lace made of spinning violets / forming a violet heart."

Almost voiceless, I said: "Faride, my daughter, what is happening to you?" I didn't even dare touch her, I sensed her distant and alien.

"Nothing is the matter, Mama."

"Where do you get these stories from?"

"What stories?"

"The ones you've just told me, the ones from breakfast on Saturday and Sunday."

"They're not stories. I wrote that poetry fifty years ago. It's mine. I don't tell stories, I never could learn any."

"Are you telling me that these are truths, reality?"

"What is the truth, Mama? What is reality?"

"The truth is the truth, the same truth you learned when you were a child. Reality is that you're twenty-three years old. You couldn't have written anything fifty years ago. Tell me the truth; you never lied."

"I'm not lying."

"Don't drive me to despair. Trust me; tell me what's happening in your life."

"I trust you. Nothing is happening to me; I am well."

"Tell me then, why are you inventing these extravagant stories so detrimental to your good name?"

"What extravagant stories?"

"These fantasies of men and love affairs so different from your reality as a serious woman."

"What is reality, Mama?"

"Reality is eating rice and plantains, giving birth to a child, working, seeing clearly what things are like!"

"And what are things like?"

I didn't insist anymore; this senseless conversation was driving me mad.

The next day, she sat at the table, giddy. The children had left for school. One of our older children was with us. I had asked him to be there, knowing that Faride respected him almost more than she did her father, she feared him more. From the time she was very young we entrusted her care to her brother. His presence, however, didn't inhibit her.

"It was a beautiful, but at the same time, boring trip; two months at sea, seeing sky, seeing blue and more blue, seeing the same people, the unseasonal birds hovering over our heads. But it was worth it. My mother's friends were waiting for me, with a bouquet of flowers and open arms. I went with Ferita to register at the university. I took only two courses: botany and history, because I first must grow used to the city and my new friends, before I throw myself completely into my studies. I get my teachers confused; they are so white, so similar. God made white people's skin with the same roll of fabric. Yesterday we went to see Unamuno's *Shadows of Dreams*. The theater is very elegant, and so are the people. After the performance we went to my apartment, we drank wine and beer, we danced, and rolled on the floor."

"Enough!" I said with anger and sadness. My oldest son only commented, "What is she talking about?" We had to practically push him out of the house by force, he was furious and wanted to beat her up. According to him, Faride had become a trollop and two or three good blows would straighten her out. She didn't seem surprised, and when we returned she even added:

"The trolley cars, the buildings, the beautiful paintings in the museums, the Graf Zeppelin, the romantic friends reciting verses in the parks."

The narratives at breakfast became routine. They sent us away from the table, they made us run out to school, they separated us from her and her belongings, managing thereby to sharpen our curiosity. We spied on conversations, searched her purse, and eluded Mama's and Papa's watchful eyes to be with her. Mama thought that Faride's ravings were a passing thing, attributing them to lack of news from Raúl.

In effect, there had been no news from him since he had left. Mama had gone to the group that had organized the trip, but they said they weren't responsible for people after they took them over. Papa considered Raúl a scoundrel; he wasn't interested in his whereabouts, and even less in his fate. That Saturday, Faride came in to the kitchen, trembling: there was a somber expression on her face. Papa and Mama were alarmed.

"It was alive, the desiccated bird, the prehistoric desiccated bird sent to me by my friend from India was alive. It chased me into the rice bog, into the labyrinth of caves in San Juan, between my legs. It seemed dead when it arrived through the mail, but it was alive. An atrocious bird, sticky, with long legs and long sharp goads instead of feathers. It was humid and dead and moved. I don't know what to do with it. I tried throwing it out the window only to find it again under my bed. Ten times I took it out of my room and it would return to my side, like an amulet reeking of death, and it is in my room, and it holds its viscous skin to my face. Oh God, it has made me throw up my insides!"

Papa and Mama listened to her in consternation. Even we, spying through the gaps in the kitchen wall, were profoundly impressed. She suddenly changed her expression and laughed:

"Ah, but what a beautiful little house. He sent it to me as a gift. It came in the mail today. It's not taller than my legs, but it has a thousand little doors, all pink, all painted in a different pink. A thousand shades of pink on the façade. When you open a little door, you find a three-verse poem and a painting which explains that year's history. A thousand years of Indian history in a thousand paintings and a thousand poems. In the last little door, the one in a pink so intense it approaches the orange of red-tinted clouds, is the Salt March and the Peace Poem: Peace, salt, autumn splendor / they are within us and together they will sprout / like a water spring that blinds certain fires."

When we, intrigued, asked her about the little house, she told us that she would show it to us later. In India, she told us, children didn't use books to study history, but little houses like these. Through millennia, Hindus have learned the exceptional art of miniaturizing trees and history.

On Faride's birthday her colleagues at work organized a little party for her, to which they invited us. We went to the store in the afternoon, after the shop closed, feeling apprehensive. To our surprise, the celebration proceeded quite normally. The shop owner gave her a certificate commending her for her exceptional performance as a salesperson; he also gave her a small gold chain, exhorting her to keep up the good work with her usual cordiality and efficiency. Her co-workers loved and admired her, as we could attest to.

At home, however, the modifications in her conduct were marked. She knitted less and spent long periods of time in silence.

She didn't waste any chance to play. She would get lost in the ring around the rosie, pocket full of posies, look who's here Punchinella, Punchinella, Miss Mary Mack Mack with silver buttons all down her back back; she ran and jumped with boundless energy, and none of us could catch her when we played tag. Papa and Mama rested easy when they saw us like that. But a turn in the situation agitated the entire household, and from then on our parents didn't even bother to hide their anguish from us.

It was Sunday. Papa was playing dominoes with a group of friends in front of the house. Faride, euphoric, started to turn around the playing table, jumping as she held the edges of her skirt, opening it like a fan. She sang out the words, heaping them onto each other in an easy flowing laughter.

"My lover returned from the crystal house. He has brought me his riddles once more. This time I will guess the answers. The glass house is celebrating tonight, all the windows have been opened and the rooms are bursting with full moons. We are going to Moscow to ride the Ferris wheel. He amuses himself with the trapeze artists. Together we built a sculpture to the tenderness of the panda bear / Providence shines like a firefly in the Caribbean Sea / with the fishermen on the golden beach / at dawn / we encircle its waters / with boreal ribbons / we wove a basket / that knows about Ithaca / through eternal ice / we go animatedly / on expeditions / silver camels / carry us on their rumps / through snowy peaks / so clear / so beautiful / that in their translucency / time melts / and the soul dissolves."

From that moment on, our household was in an upheaval. Faride would tell her rapturous stories to anyone who would listen. Some people would come to our house and incite her to talk so as to feed the rumors circulating around the neighborhood. Mama and Papa quickly gathered together some money and took her to a psychiatrist.

He examined her and submitted her to different tests. He tested her reflexes, laid logical traps for her; they spoke for more than an hour. Faced with our bewilderment, he told us she was undoubtedly sane, and that he found her to be an intelligent and cooperative young woman. We narrated to him the events of Sunday and of the days before. He asked us to understand her youth and her ideas. The dreams of each generation differ, he insisted. I insisted on his hearing her in front of us, thinking that perhaps she had pulled the wool over his eyes. We called her in and I asked her to read one of her poems. She then proceeded to recite with great spontaneity, looking us in the eye:

"Populations of stars uninhabit the sky to hurl themselves at my heavens / matrixes of fresh bubbles / pay deaf ears to their original water springs / and make a watery bouquet in my sex / juice of virgin meadows / squeezed by sheer will / form the blood of my wanderings / I am with them / a game of love / a born traveler."

The doctor expressed that that poetry confirmed his diagnosis: Faride was intelligent and original, and he advised us to let her be. We left his office even more baffled; no one said a word on our way back.

Her dreams gained ground as the days went by. It was hard to wake her up in the morning. Sometimes she would wash up, have breakfast in the kitchen, and return to bed. We would wake her up again by shaking her roughly. She would do two or three routine chores and then return to bed to continue her interrupted sleep. When we forced her to get up and kept her from returning to bed, as I lectured her on her lack of responsibility toward work and of the importance of her salary to the family's finances, she would walk through the house as if it were a stage and she the leading actress, playing a role known only to herself.

Sometimes, sitting upright in bed, she examined her surroundings as if she didn't recognize anything. She walked by inertia, repeating to us previous dialogues. Pensive and inexpressive, it would take her up to three-quarters of an hour to cross the line that divided her two realities.

We did all we could to isolate the neighbors from the atmosphere of our house. Our older children would entertain visitors in front of the house, taking chairs out to the sidewalk and engaging in conversation almost on the street. I abstained from going out. I went only to mass on Sunday and I tried to do so with the greatest discretion: I was terrified of questions. We forbade the children to enter Faride's bedroom. After repeated excuses, we had to admit that she wouldn't return to work, and so we informed the shop owner. But all our efforts did nothing more than unleash more rumors. The neighbors' assumptions were like knives in my heart. As far as they were concerned Faride was pregnant, Faride had had a botched abortion in a back-alley clinic, Faride had an unstoppable hemorrhage, Faride had gone mad and walked naked through the house making pornographic gestures, Faride was rotting with cancer, her face had been eaten up by maggots, and, therefore, we had locked her up.

Our friends asked us in school if it was true that our sister smelled bad, if we were having another little brother or sister, how many men had given her children; they asked us if we would get sick just like her. Faced with that rosary of rumors, Mama drastically changed policies. She opened doors and windows, invited the neighboring women to the house for coffee, canceled the orders that kept us away from our sister, allowed her children to sleep with her again, and no longer prevented her from going out into the yard.

The friends and neighbors saw her walk the sidewalk, water the eggplants planted in the yard, and frolic with her children. They took turns spying on her, since she would let herself be seen only once in a while. Some ended up attributing to her a passing illness or a harmless dementia. They also agreed, however, that her physique did not betray any ailment whatsoever. They saw her like she looked then: her profile more defined, her cheeks rosy and with a profound calm always peeking through her eyes.

Every once in a while I would sit down to watch her sleep. Certain discoveries had awakened in me hopes of a cure. Watching her fixedly, I noticed the movements of her eyelids and the slight stretching of her lips when the familiar voices of the market women offered their pigeon peas, coriander, and oregano for sale. She didn't seem disconnected from the prattle of children playing baseball in the neighborhood park. If my daughter was not completely rooted in this reality, neither was she in the other.

Mama's hopes soon began to fade. Faride's residence on this side of reality diminished progressively, until it was reduced to the narrow space of no more than an hour. Then she would awaken completely, drink a glass of water, bathe and perfume herself. She would talk briefly with Mama and Papa and would romp with us for a while, demonstrating a complete command of her two diverse time frames. When she was asleep, she lay totally submerged in a deep tranquility; when she was awake, she was nimble and clear-sighted.

One day she awakened all of us with a frantic cry. It was a calm dawn in April, fresh and fragrant. I will never forget it. Standing around her bed, we heard her last words.

"I have found the solution! Kiss me all of you!! Kiss me and hold me in your arms because I have found the solution!! Now I know how to irrigate a garden that won't stop growing, how to gather the shadows of the flowers, how to prevent their concealing the sun, and how to walk diagonally across the instants."

She went to sleep definitively. She slept for exactly six months. Pale, on her back, smiling: her heartbeats began to fade. At the end she looked like a beautiful dream dressed in pink, a dream that our parents refused to bury.

I don't know why the family opted for the diagnosis of madness. The notion that it was a singular form of dementia, still unexplored by psychiatry, is taking root in José; his career plans are driven by the desire to deepen the investigation of the case.

The one exception is the mother, for whom the daughter was possessed by a woman from the past; her eagerness leads her to think that José, sometimes, is possessed by Faride's spirit. They alone knew her intimately, having witnessed every detail of the most intense moments of her extraordinary behavior; but they could be mistaken, however, and it could perhaps be a mere matter of poetics.

Translated by Lizabeth Paravisini-Gebert.
From Volume 6: Pleasure in the Word

ROMELIA ALARCÓN DE FOLGAR

PROTEST

Why remember that I am a poet
and that wild flowers
grow daily on my chest.

In the enclosed circle of the day
any sound touches my heart
and even the asphalt on the streets frightens me.

A few weeks ago I wrote a poem
a son of mine made of the earth and the sky
I sent him to the newspaper,
I have heard no more of him
he is out of focus.

Maybe he is lost
among a bundle of papers
that talk about murders,
the raped girl,
politics, expensive lives
and many other things where there is no room
for either a rose or love.

He, that son of mine, was only carrying
by way of provisions a handful of grass
and a few odd stars
in his pockets.
Because
it was
poor equipment
he would feel defenseless and alone
he was lacking a dagger and a machine gun.

Poetry is in exile
nobody wants anything to do with her.
Her plumed robes
are useless
if there are unburied men
abandoned on the streets.

Translated by Alison Ridley.
From Volume 7: *These Are Not Sweet Girls*

ALFONSINA STORNI

TO MY LADY OF POETRY

I throw myself here at your feet, sinful,
my dark face against your blue earth,
you the virgin among armies of palm trees
that never grow old as humans do.

I don't dare look at your pure eyes
or dare touch your miraculous hand:
I look behind me and a river of rashness
urges me guiltlessly on against you.

With a promise to mend my ways through your
divine grace, I humbly place on your
hem a little green branch,

for I couldn't have possibly lived
cut off from your shadow, since you blinded me
at birth with your fierce branding iron.

Translated by Kay Short.
From Volume 1: *Alfonsina Storni: Selected Poems*

CRISTINA PERI ROSSI

FROM EVOHÉ

Tired of women
of the terrible stories they told me,
tired of the flesh,
its tremblings and yearnings,
like a hermit,
I took refuge in words.

A woman dances in my ears
words from childhood
I listen to her
calmly look at her
am looking at her ceremoniously
and if she says smoke
if she says fish caught in our bare hands,
says my father and my mother and my siblings
I feel something undefined
slipping from antiquity
a molasses of words
for, while she speaks,
she has conquered me
holding me like this,
hooked to her letters
syllables and consonants
as if I had penetrated her.
She has me hooked
whispering to me ancient things
things I've forgotten
things that never existed
but now, when pronounced,
become facts,
and while she speaks to me she takes me to bed

where I wouldn't want to go
because of the sweetness of the word *come*.

When she opens her mouth and doesn't sigh
but delicately goes threading letters,
an *o* here, an *a* over there,
that fine consonant sharp as a needle,
light as a feather
and when she has finished a pretty phrase
she flings it into the air
and we all line up to watch it
to observe its qualities
for she has so well combined the sounds
the colors
one would think her a poet
laying words out with harmony
making them sound so well
and I think that just like her periods
her shoulders
her breasts must ring
and damned if I don't begin to think on the music
her legs will make
and how her hair will tremble
shaken in the trill
and how her hands will vibrate in the melopoeia
then with an ax I destroy the piano.

to write
to eat
to go to the movies
to listen to any music
to sleep
to keep vigil
to stroll by statues
to set myself up in a house
to get a cat

to buy a much-needed piece of furniture,
to never leave the city,
the country,
naturally, to make poetry,
naturally, to believe in the woman,
to love her an entire day
and then, dissatisfied,
to love other women,
to leave her love for another's
to tell stories,
and among those stories,
to tell this story,
to die a few more days,
and perhaps—if we get along well—
to die even some years.

Translated by Diana P. Decker.
From Volume 7: *These Are Not Sweet Girls*

Delmira Agustini

The Ineffable

I am dying in a strange way...Life is not killing me,
Death is not killing me, Love is not killing me;
I am dying of a thought as mute as a wound...
Have you never felt the strange pain

of an immense thought that takes root in your life,
devouring soul and flesh, and not coming into bloom?
Have you never borne within you a sleeping star
that burned all through you and never showed its glow?

Pinnacle of Martydoms!...To eternally bear
the tragic seed, the wrenching and arid seed,
sunk into your guts like a ferocious tooth!...

Yet to pluck it out one day as a flower
that would open miraculous and inviolable...Ah,
it would be no greater to have in one's hand the head of God!

Translated by Mark McCaffrey.
From Volume 7: *These Are Not Sweet Girls*

Idéa Vilareño

No

I shouldn't write this
shouldn't sit here
suffering
feeling
the horror of the void
letting myself
this
become vertigo
nausea.
I really should look away
really should laugh it off
once and for all
let it be.

Translated by Louise B. Popkin.
From Volume 7: *These Are Not Sweet Girls*

CLEMENTINA SUÁREZ

THE POEM

If you start to write a poem
think first of who will read it.
Because a rhyme is only a rhyme
when someone understands it and lives on
over and above all,
having escaped the mediocrity
that flippancy or wordiness exalts.

A poem is not necessarily as it is
but as it should be in its spirit of justice.
A word is sufficient to love hope
and to speak of this is more important
than the most beautiful but ordinary poem.

Translated by Janet N. Gold.
From Volume 7: These Are Not Sweet Girls

Julia de Burgos

I Have Lost a Verse

Swallowing the dark truths at my sides
in the silent night I permitted the loss of a verse.

Each truth implored the statue of words
which quickly engraved my active thought;
and not to belong to everyone with impetus of bird,
through the door which it came ran away my verse.

In it there was no desire to raise up emotions
tired and small expressed at the moment,
and dragging life, undid its brief age
and removed itself from the verbal world of my brain.

It left silently, deformed and mutilated,
carrying in its muteness the vague feeling
of having dressed in flesh wasted by words
to exhibit my entrance as a poetic attempt.
       You! Verse!
             In you is made the life of another mind,
of another strange anxiety, of another pain.
                            You! Verse!
I have here the great scenario which in your look of bird
deformed and mutilated by not entering in my eaves,
you will see rise up, on a shaft of dumb horizons
disappearing below knowing themselves small:

Four streets of men. Four streets square
deeds of the outside sun with impulse toward the inside.

Believers taciturn moving themselves twisted
in the static of four right angles.

Value of water stanched in the not being of centuries
that died of inertia beneath its own weight.

Value of man squared cowering humble
to drown himself in the waters with torpor of slave.

You! Verse!
In you man did not make himself; nor the centuries.
The static has broken itself in your song.
                                                    You! Verse!

You have returned to the vibrant definition of form
that you warmed at the shadow of the first impulse.

Now I can define you. You bring impetus of idea,
and in your words vibrates the rhythm of the new.

You are the today of the world: the affirmation; the
strength.
Revolution that breaks the curtain of time!

In your Being, inevitable revolution of the world,
I have found myself on having found my verse.

Translated by Heather Rosario Sievert.
From Volume 7: These Are Not Sweet Girls

NANCY MOREJÓN

REQUIEM FOR THE LEFT HAND

For Marta Valdés

All kinds of lines can be traced on a map,
    horizontal, straight, diagonal,
from the Greenwich Meridian to the Gulf of Mexico
    lines that more or less
reflect our idiosyncrasy

there are also very large maps
    in the imagination
and infinite terrestrial globes
    Marta

but today I guess that on a very
    small map
the smallest
drawn on notebook paper
    all of history can fit
eveything

CARPET

Without warning, the idea of the poem
enters through the window,
perhaps, with a scent.
By chance was it able to deceive so many misguided longings...?
It is as if
someone would slip a carpet under my feet
and on solid ground, I might begin
a new flight, I as benevolent as
that reader whose dream cherished
Boti's reading...
I can't...
Oh unshaken dream
oh clear sails coming toward my red body...
And the idea of the poem
is no longer here,
is no longer here.

Translated by Joy Renjilian-Burgy.
From Volume 7: These Are Not Sweet Girls

CECILIA VICUÑA

FROM PALABRAMÁS

I saw a word in the air
solid and suspended
showing me
her seed body

She opened up and fell apart
and from her parts sprouted
sleeping thoughts
        of love, livid
                in love, living
                out of love
came madder violet

Enchanting me
nipples and cupolas
chanting in me

She ascends in a spiral
as I fall in the break
between chant and cupola

In and out
of deserted palaces I wander
seeing the image of chanting
and entering
the beginning
        the end
           the word

The fractal image has thighs
hips and wounds

to enter

She is mother and wind
her lean body
stalks and waits

She seeks
the door
whistling in love
pushing it
with a terse blow as
the door rolls
                    in place

No one will see the same palace
once the threshold has been crossed
no one will see the same flowers
except through the gift
of ubiquity

Coincidence is a miracle
of chance, the crossing
of two vectors,
carelessly placed perhaps

Each word
awaits the traveler
hoping to find
in her
trails and suns
of thought

They wait
singing in silence
one hundred times touched

and changed
exhausted for a moment
and then revived

Lost or abandoned
they shine again

Celestial bodies
each
in its orbit

Quartz structure
sensed by touch
and the inner ear

Body music
forms transform
born to die
enjoying
their conjugation

Space
that we penetrate

Lords of pen
in trance

Lords of words
or do they
love our works?

Do they
desire us as we
desire them?

Translated by Suzanne Jill Levine.
From Volume 7: *These Are Not Sweet Girls*

WORDS

We wait for the rain to stop. For the winds to come. We speak. For the love of silence we utter useless words. A pained, painful utterance, without escape, for the love of silence, for love of the body's language. I would speak; language has always been an excuse for silence. It's my way of expressing my unspeakable weariness.

This fatal order of things should be reversed. Words should be used to seduce the one we love, but through pure silence. I have always been the silent one. Now I use those mediating words I have heard so much. But who has so often praised lovers over those loved? My deepest leaning: to the edge of silence. The mediation of words, the lure of language. This is my life now: self-restraint, trembling at every voice, tempering words by calling upon all the cursed and fatal things that I have heard and read about the ways of seduction.

The fact is, I enumerated, analyzed and compared the examples gathered from my readings or from mutual friends. I could show that I was right, that love was right. I promised him that if he loved me, a place of perfect justice would be his. But I wasn't in love with him; I only wanted to be loved by him and no one else. It's so hard to talk about. When I saw his face for the first time, I wanted it to turn toward mine out of love. I wanted his eyes to fall deeply into mine. Of this I wish to speak. Of a love that's impossible because there is no love. A love story without love. I speak too soon. There is love. There's love in the same way that I went out the other night and observed: there's wind tonight. Not a story without love. Or rather, a story about substitutes.

There are gestures that pierce me between the legs: a fear and a shuddering in my genitals. Seeing his face pause for a fraction of a second, his face frozen for an immeasurable moment, his face, such a dead stop, like the change in one's voice when saying no. That Dylan Thomas poem about the hand signing the page. A face that lasts as long as a hand signing a name on a sheet of paper. I felt it in my genitals. Levitation: I am lifted, I fly. A *no*, because of that *no* everything comes undone. I have to give an orderly account of this disorder. A disorderly accounting of this strange order of things. While *no* goes on and on.

I speak of an approaching poem. It comes closer as I am held at a distance. Weariness without rest, untiring weariness as night—not a poem—approaches and I am beside him and nothing, nothing happens as night draws near, passes by and nothing, nothing happens. Only a very distant voice, a magical belief, an absurd, ancient wait for better things.

Not long ago I said *no* to him. An unspeakable transgression. I said no, when for months I've died waiting. When I begin the gesture, when I began... A shaking shudder, hurting, wounding myself, thirsting for excess (thinking sometime about the importance of the syllable *no*).

Translated by Suzanne Jill Levine.
From Volume 6: *Pleasure in the Word*

IN THIS NIGHT, IN THIS WORLD

To Martha Isabel Moia

in this night in this world
the words of the dream of childhood of death
that is never what one wants to say
the native tongue castrates
the tongue is an organ of cognition
of the failure of every poem
castrated by its own tongue
which is the organ of re-creation
of re-cognition
but not of resurrection
of something like negation
of my horizon of maldoror with his dog
and nothing is promise
among the expressible
which is the same as lying
(everything that can be said is a lie)
the rest is silence
except silence doesn't exist

no
words
don't make love
they make absence
if I say *water*, am I drinking?
if I say *bread*, am I eating?

in this night in this world
extraordinary the silence of this night
what is happening with the soul is that it's not seen
what is happening with the mind is that it's not seen
what is happening with the spirit is that it's not seen

where does this conspiracy of invisibilities come from?
no word is visible
shadows
viscous enclosures
where the stone of folly hides
black hallways
I have gone through them all
oh, stay among us a little longer!

my person is wounded
my first person singular

I write like someone with a knife raised in darkness
I write like I am saying
absolute sincerity would continue being
the impossible
oh, stay among us a little longer!

the wearing out of words
deserting the palace of language
cognition between the legs
what did I do with the gift of sex?
oh my dead ones
I ate them up I choked
I can't stand not being able to stand it

muffles words
everything slides
toward the black liquification
and maldoror's dog
in this night in this world
where everything is possible
except
poems
I speak
knowing it's not about that

always it's not about that
oh help me write the most dispensable poem
        the one that can't be used
        even to be useless
help me write words
in this night in this world

Translated by María Rosa Fort and Frank Graziano.
From Volume 6: *Pleasure in the Word*

THE AUTHORS

MARJORIE AGOSÍN (Chile, 1955) has lived in exile in the United States since 1970. A prolific writer, she is also well-known for her work as a human rights activist. Her recent work includes *Happiness* (1993), *Starry Night* (1996), *Ashes of Revolt: Essays on Human Rights* (1997), *A Cross and a Star* (1995), and *Always from Somewhere Else: A Memoir of My Chilean Jewish Father* (1998). She is the editor of White Pine Press' acclaimed Secret Weavers Series: Writing by Latin American Women. She lives in Massachustetts, where she is professor of Spanish at Wellesley College.

ROSARIO AGUILAR (Nicaragua, 1938) has written seven novels and two biographical narratives. Her work focuses on female characters, both real and imaginary, and on the social, political, economic, and psychological realities that vex women in Western society. Her works include *Primavera sonámbula* (1964), *Las doce y veintinueve* (1975), *Aguel mar sin fondo ni playa* (1970), *El guerrillero* (1976), *Siete relatos sobre el amor y la guerra* (1986) and *La niña blanca y los pájaros sin pies*, published in English as *The Lost Chronicles of Terra Firma* (1997).

DELMIRA AGUSTINI (Uruguay, 1886-1914) studied music and languages at home and began to write literary reviews in 1902. She published her first book of poetry, *El libro blanco* in 1907 and just two more volumes in her lifetime: *Cantos de la mañana* (1910) and *Los cálices vacíos* (1913). The rest of her work was published in two volumes ten years after she was murdered by her ex-husband: *Los astros del abismo* and *El rosario de Eros*. One of Latin America's most experimental writers, she is considered to be the initiator of erotic poetry in Latin America.

ROMELIA ALCAROÑ DE FOLGAR (Guatemala, 1920-1970) was both a poet and a journalist. Among her works are *Claridad* (1960) and *Tiempo inmovil* (1965).

DORA ALONSO (Cuba, 1910) wrote for Cuban national radio and television for many years. "Tierra Brava," Cuba's wildly-popular television soap opera, is based on her novel, *Media Luna*. She is also the author of *Tierra adentro* (1944) and *Tierra inerme* (1961) as well as numerous short stories, plays, and children's books.

GIOCONDA BELLI (Nicaragua, 1948) received the Casa de las Américas prize for her poetry collection, *Línea del fuego*. Her novel, *La mujer habitada,* won the prize for best literary work of the year from the Union of German Publishers and Editors. Her work in English includes *From Eve's Rib* and *The Inhabited Woman*.

MARTA BLANCO (Chile, 1938) is a professor of journalism at the Catholic University in Santiago and a short story writer, as well as novelist. Her first novel, *La generacion de las hojas*, made an important contribution to Chilean feminism. In 1974, she published *Todo es mentira*, a collection of short stories, and in 1988 she published a collection of interviews of distinguished literary figures.

MARTA BRUNET (Chile, 1897-1967) was considered, along with María Luisa Bombal, to be one of the most distinguished writers of her generation. Her writing powerfully depicts the plight of rural women in Chile. Her works include *Bestia Dañia* (1953), *Aguas agajo* (1943), and *Cuentos para Marisol* (1966).

TERESA CALDERÓN (Chile, 1955) studied American literature at the University of Chile. Considered one of Latin America's best contemporary poets, she has been awarded numerous prizes, among them the Fundacioñ Neruda Prize for Poetry. Her work includes *Causa peridida* (1984).

ROSARIO CASTELLANOS' (MEXICO, 1925-1974) impressive list of publications includes two novels, *Balún-Canán*

(1957), which deals with the exploitation of the Indians, and *Oficio de tinieblas* (1962); three volumes of short stories, including *Álbum de familia* (1971); four collections of essays and criticism, among them *Mujer que sabe latín* (1973); several plays, chief among them *El eterno femenino* (1975); and a dozen books of poems, which have been collected under the titles *Poesía no eres tú* (1972) and *Meditación en el umbral* (1985). Her work is marked by her concern with the many varieties of domination prevalent in Latin American socieites. She died in an automobile accident in Tel Aviv, where she was living as Mexican ambassador to Israel.

JULIA DE BURGOS (Puerto Rico, 1914-1953) wrote poetry characterized by her defense of the working class and of her feminist and nationalist ideals. Her three collections of poetry are *Poema en veinte surcos* (1938), *Canción de la verdad sencilla* (1939), and *El mar y tú* (1954). Her work is credited as helping to undermine the male-oriented aspects of traditional Puerto Rican culture and with broadening the range of Puerto Rican literature to include women's experience.

ROSARIO FERRÉ (PUERTO RICO, 1938) was educated in the U.S. and holds a Ph.D. in Hispanic languages and literature from the University of Maryland. She was editor of *Zona de cargada y descargada*, a literary magazine which introduced feminist inquiry into the study of literature in the Spanish-speaking world. Ferré writes poetry, novels, short stories, and literary criticism. Her first books, *Papeles de Pandora* (1976), *Sitio a Eros* (1980), and *Fábulas de la garza desangrada* (1982) were all critically acclaimed, as was her first novel, *Maldito amor* (1986), which she translated into English herself, thus establishing herself as an accomplished bilingual writer. Her work has consistently explored the role of women in Puerto Rican society, questioning the feminine stereotypes common in Latin America and pointing to their roots in the class system.

ALAIDE FOPPA (Guatemala, 1913-1980), a leading feminist and one of Guatemala's best writers, taught at the University of Mexico. She returned to Guatemala in 1980 at the age of sixty-seven to visit her ailing mother. While in Guatemala City, she was kidnapped and never seen again. It is presumed that she was murdered by the government. An essayist and poet, she was the author of five collections of poetry. Her principal works include *Aunque es la noche* (1959), *Los dedos de mi mano* (1972) and *La sin ventura* (1975).

SARA GALLARDO (Argentina, 1934-1988) worked as a journalist in the 1950s, traveling and writing extensively in Latin America, Europe, and the Orient. She wrote several novels dealing with marginal areas in Southern Argentina and the Patagonia. In her narrative, the landscape acquires a new, mythical element, as do the people who live in it. Among her works are *Enero* (1958), *El país de humo* (1987) and *Páginas de Sara Gallardo* (1987).

MAGALI GARCÍA RAMIS (Puerto Rico, 1946) began her litereray career in 1971 with the publication of "Todos los domingos," which won first prize at the Ateneo de Puerto Rico short story contest. She has written for magazines, journals and newspapers, with her themes reflecting everyday situations and containing abundant social commentary and criticism. In 1972 she helped found the School of Public Communication at the University of Puerto Rico and has taught and held administrative positions there since. Her publications include *Felices días tío Sergio* ((1986; English translation 1995), *Las horas del sur*, and *Las noches del Riel de Oro*.

MARCELA GUIJOSA (MEXICO, 1945) is a journalist in Mexico City and a collaborator on the magazine *Fem*, one of Mexico's most important feminist magazines. She is the author of *Altar de muertos*, a memoir about being mestiza. A professor at the National University of Mexico City, she has also written numerous essays and books of poetry.

ANA MARÍA GUIRALDES (Chile, 1945) studied Latin American literture at the Catholic University of Santiago. Her first published works were children's stories, for which she won numerous prizes. She then turned to adult novels. Her published work includes *El sueño de María Soledad* (1973), *El sola* (1984), *Cuentos de soledad y asombro* (1991) and *El castillo negro en el deserto* (1994).

LILIANA HEKER (Argentina, 1943) has been a successful writer in her native Argentina since she was a teenager. Although Argentina's military governments have oppressed and even murdered dissenters, Heker urged her colleagues not to flee to safety, remaining behind herself to edit the literary journal *El Ornitorrinco* (The Platypus). Her works include *Those Who Beheld the Burning Bush* and *Zona de Clivage*, which won the Buenos Aires Municipal Prize in 1989.

ÁNGELA HERNÁNDEZ (Dominican Republic, 1954) was trained in chemical engineering but has worked primarily as a researcher and activist on women's issues. Known primarily as a poet and essayist—she has published two volumes of poetry and numerous essays on feminism and women's rights—Hernández published her first collection of short stories, *Alótropos*, in 1989. Her work is characterized by the poetic richness of her prose and by her blending of vivid details of the external world with a poet's understanding of the fantastic world of the imagination.

MARTA JARA (Chile, 1919-1972) was an important Chilean writer of short stories and one of the first women to participate in the *criollista* movement. She was a friend of Pablo Neruda and collaborated with him in an important literary magazine, *La gaceta literaria*. She won ma ny important awards and prizes for her work, including the Municipal Prize for Literature.

Among her works are *El vaquero de dios* (1949) and *Surazo* (1962).

ILKE BRUNHILDE LAURITO (Brazil, 1925) is a poet and professor of literature in Sao Paulo. Laurito has also participated in the production of television programs on Brazil for the BBC in London. Her collections include *A Noiva do Horizonte* (1953), *Autobiografia de Maos Dadas* (1958), *Janela de Apartamento* (1968), *Sol do Lírico* (1978), and *Genetrix* (1982).

BELKIS CUZA MALÉ (Cuba, 1942) was born in Oriente province but later moved to Havana, where she worked as a journalist. She emigrated to the U.S. in the 1970s, where she worked as editor of *Linden Lane* magazine. Among her books are *Los alucinados*, *Tiempo del sol*, *Cartas a Ana Frank*, *El clavel y la Rosa* and *Women on the Front Lines*.

GABRIELA MISTRAL (Chile, 1889-1957) was the first Latin American writer to win the Nobel Prize for Literature. During her young adulthood, she worked as a teacher, counting among her students a young Pablo Neruda. Her poetic career began in earnest in 1914 when "Los sonetos de la muerte" won the Chilean national prize for poetry. After years spent traveling in Latin America and Europe, she settled in the U.S. for the final years of her life. Her work includes *Desolación* (1922), *Ternura* (1924), *Tala* (1938), and *Lagar* (1954). The first English-language collection of both her poems and prose work appeared in the U.S. in 1993.

NANCY MOREJÓN (Cuba, 1944) studied French literature at the University of Havana and has translated Paul Eluard, Aimé Césaire and Jacques Roumain into Spanish. Her poetry is committed to the Cuban revolution and gives voice to oppressed groups while striving for political empowerment and social justice. In addition, they rescue her anonymous African ancestors from oblivion and reflect on her extended Caribbean family.

She resides in Havana, where she works at the Fundación Pablo Milanés. Her books of poetry include *Mutismos* (1962), *Amor, ciudad atribuida* (1964), *Richard trajo su flauta* (1967), *Piedra pulida* (1986), *Parajes de una época* (1979), *Octubre imprescindible* (1982), and *Cuaderno de Granada* (1984).

CARMEN NARANJO (Costa Rica, 1931) served as her country's ambassador to Israel in the 1970s. She has also served as the cultural minister of Costa Rica and developed the country's system of social security. Best known as a novelist, her works include *Cancion de la ternura* (1964) and *My Guerilla* (1966).

CRISTINA PACHECO (MEXICO, 1948) was born in Mexico City and began working as a journalist, where she took a special interest in issues of social justice. She has written for all of Mexico City's major newspapers and is the author of *Sopa de fideos*, a collection of oral histories about Mexico's poor.

ALEJANDRA PIZARNIK (Argentina, 1936-1972) published eight books of poetry before her suicide. Among them are *La tierra más ajena* (1955), *La última inocencia* (1956), *Los trabajos y las noches* (1965), *Extracción de la piedras de la locura* (1968), and *Nombres y figuras* (1969), *El infierno musical* (1971) and a biography of Countess Erzbet Bathory, *La condesa sangrienta* (1971). A permanent reflection on writing, a permanent inquisition into the nature of poetry, guides her work. She posits a subject in constant quest for her identity amidst fragmented voices that never fully name her, a poetic "I" who makes love to words and is destroyed by them. Pizarnik displayed a surprising, unrestrained imagination in her work, which is often charactrized by an unsettling view of reality and a macabre fictional landscape.

GIOVANNA POLLAROLO (Peru, 1955) is considered to be one of the most innovative poets currently writing in Latin America. She studied to be an elementary school teacher in Tacna in northern Peru, then settled in Lima, where she studied literature at the Catholic University. She has written movie scripts, including *La boca del loso* (1988) and *Caidos del cielo* (1989). She teaches at the University of the Pacific in Lima and is also a journalist. Her first collection of poems *Entre mujeres solas* sold out its entire print run a few weeks after its publication in 1991.

ELENA PONIATOWSKA (MEXICO, 1933), born in Paris the daughter of a Polish count and a Mexican aristocrat, has sought to give voice in her works to the marginalized and politically voiceless. A journalist by trade, she has received high praise for her courageous and innovative testimonial works, among them *La noche de Tlatelolco* (1971). Her powerful novel, *Hasta no verte, Jesús mío*, recounts the life story of a woman who followed the army to provide food, drink, care, and other services to the soldiers during the Mexican Revolution. In *Querido Diego*, she imagines the feelings, hopes, and final despair of one of Diego de Rivera's mistresses, a painter who agonizes in poverty and loneliness in Paris after Diego has left for Mexico. Poniatowska's 1988 novel, *Flor de lis*, is considered to be largely autobiographical.

AMALIA RENDIC (Chile, 1928-1988) is considered to be one of the most outstanding Latin American writers of children's literature. She also wrote one novel for adults, *Pasos Sonambulos* (1969). Rendic lived in northern Chile, which was the inspiration for much of her work. She taught French literature at the Catholic University of Santiago. Among her works are *Hierto amargo* (1960), *Los pasos sonámbulos* (1975), and *Portal de luna* (1979).

LAURA RIESCO (Peru, 1940), born in the Andes, came to the U.S. to complete her university studies. She resides in Maine, where she taught, until her recent retirement, at the University of Maine. Her work includes *El truco de los ojos* (1978) and *Ximena de dos caminos* (*Ximena at the Crossroads*) (1994; English translation, 1998). The best-selling book in Peru's history, *Ximena at the Crossroads* was honored in Peru as Best Novel of the Year and Best Prose Written by a Woman, both in 1994. The book also won the 1995 Latino Prize in Literature for fiction.

CRISTINA PERI ROSSI (Uruguay, 1941) was active in the left-wing resistance to military oppression in her country and was forced to flee in 1972 to exile in Barcelona, where she writes and works as a journalist. Her work embodies a radical questioning of social and gender mores, literary tradition, and political structures. Her prose and poetry have been especially noted for their deep erotic sensitivity and acute imagery. Among her best-known works of poetry, fiction and essay are *Descripción de un naufragio* (1975), *Evohé* (1971, *El libro de mis primos* (1969) *La nave de los locos* (1984), and *Ship of Fools* (1989).

EMMA SEPÚLVEDA-PULVIRENTI (Argentina, 1950) had nearly completed a degree in history at the Universidad de Chile when Allende was overthrown in 1973. She fled to exile in the U.S., and later received her Ph.D. from the University of California. She teaches at the University of Nevada, Reno. Her works include *Los límites del lenguaje: un acercamiento a la poética del silencio* (1990) and *Tiempo Cómplice del tiempo* (1989). She is also an acclaimed photographer.

ALFONSINA STORNI (ARGENTINA, 1892-1938) is considered by many to be one of the greatest twentieth century poets of South America. Born in Switzerland, she was taken to Argentina as a very young child by her immigrant parents. A very visible figure in Argentine literary society, her nonconformist attitudes made her a frequent subject of controversy. She published steadily from 1916 until her suicide in 1938. Her poems reveal her intense desire for equality of the sexes and the rights of women in a time and culture unsympathetic to such aspirations. Unconventional in both her writing and her life, her feminist reputation derives from poems such as "You Want Me White" and "Little Bitty Man," in which she questions and rejects the double standard between men and women. Her books include *Irremediablemente* (1919), *Poemas de amor* (1926), and *Obra completa* (1976).

CLEMENTINA SUÁREZ (Honduras, 1906-1991) published numerous collections of poems, among them *Corazón sangranto* (1930), *Los templos del fuego* (1931), *Engranajes* (1935), and *El poeta y sus señales* (1969). She is known for her strong, sensual poetry that examines the many meanings of being a woman.

ANABEL TORRES (Colombia, 1948) is one of the most respected contemporary authors in Latin America. She has won several national poetry awards. Her books include *La mujer del esquimal* (1989) and *Las bocas del amor* (1985). She now resides in Berlin.

LUISA VALENZUELA (Argentina, 1938) has worked as a journalist and newspaper editor in her native Argentina. She has published several novels and collections of short stories, all characterized by her highly personal and ironic view of reality. Her publications include *Hay que sonreír* (1966), *Los heréticos* (1967), *El gato eficaz* (1972), *Aquí pasan cosas raras* (1975), *Cambios de armas* (1982), and *Cola de larartija* (1983). She has lived in the United States since 1979.

ANA VASQUEZ (Chile, 1945) is a Chilean sociologist and a well-known writer. She has lived in Paris since 1973. Her work deals with issues of women and human rights. When she left Chile during the Pinochet dictatorship, she became an important human rights activist. Her works include *Abel Sánchez y sus hermanos*, *Mi amiga Chantal*, and *Roch*, a novel written in collaboration with her son. Her work has beeen translated into several languages. She writes in both Spanish and French.

CECILIA VICUÑA (Chile, 1948)) began her university studies in her native Chile and continued them in Great Britain. Her poems have been published in journals in Latin America, Europe, and the United States, as well as in several collections: *Sabor a mí* (1973), *Precario/Precarious* (1983), *Luxumei o el traspie de la doctrina* (1983), *PALABRARmás* (1984), and *La Wik'uña* (1990). She lives in the U.S.

IDÉA VILAREÑO (Uruguay, 1920) is a meditative poet who masterfully puts into practice what one of her critics so aptly called "the evocative power of omission." Her voice is muted, and strives for a curiously bleak tone. Although not expressionless, it is reticent and morose, spare in its use of metaphor and suspicious of rhetorical devices. Perhaps best known for her love poems, she is also a highly-regarded translator and literary critic. Her collections include *Poemas de amor* (1957), *Nocturnos* (1951), *Treinta poemas,* (1966, and *Nocturnos del pobre amor* (1989).

THE SECRET WEAVERS SERIES

•

Series Editor: Marjorie Agosín

Dedicated to bringing the rich and varied writing
by Latin American women to the English-speaking audience.

•

Volume 13
A SECRET WEAVERS ANTHOLOGY
Edited by Andrea O'Reilly Herrera
232 pages $14.00

•

Volume 12
XIMENA AT THE CROSSROADS
A novel by Laura Riesco
Translated by Mary G. Berg
240 pages $14.00

•

Volume 11
A NECKLACE OF WORDS
Short Fiction by Mexican Women
Edited by Marjorie Agosín
152 PAGES $14.00

•

Volume 10
THE LOST CHRONICLES OF TERRA FIRMA
A Novel by Rosario Aguilar
Translated by Edward Waters Hood
192 pages $13.00

Volume 3
LANDSCAPES OF A NEW LAND
Short Fiction by Latin American Women
Edited by Marjorie Agosín
194 pages $12.00

•

Volume 1
ALFONSINA STORNI: SELECTED POEMS
Edited by Marion Freeman
72 pages $8.00

About White Pine Press

White Pine Press is a non-profit publishing house dedicated to enriching our literary heritage; promoting cultural awareness, understanding, and respect; and, through literature, addressing social and human rights issues. This mission is accomplished by discovering, producing, and marketing to a diverse circle of readers exceptional works of poetry, fiction, non-fiction, and literature in translation from around the world. Through White Pine Press, authors' voices reach out across cultural, ethnic, and gender boundaries to educate and to entertain.

To insure that these voices are heard as widely as possible, White Pine Press arranges author reading tours and speaking engagements at various colleges, universities, organizations, and bookstores throughout the country. White Pine Press works with colleges and public schools to enrich curricula and promotes discussion in the media. Through these efforts, literature extends beyond the books to make a difference in a rapidly changing world.

As a non-profit organization, White Pine Press depends on support from individuals, foundations, and government agencies to bring you this literature that matters—work that might not be published by profit-driven publishing houses. Our grateful thanks to the many individuals who support this effort as Friends of White Pine Press and to the following organizations: Amter Foundation, Ford Foundation, Korean Culture and Arts Foundation, Lannan Foundation, Lila Wallace-Reader's Digest Fund, Margaret L. Wendt Foundation, Mellon Foundation, National Endowment for the Arts, New York State Council on the Arts, Trubar Foundation, Witter Bynner Foundation, the Slovenian Ministry of Culture, The U.S.-Mexico Fund for Culture, and Wellesley College.

Please support White Pine Press' efforts to present voices that promote cultural awareness and increase understanding and respect among diverse populations of the world. Tax-deductible donations can be made to:

White Pine Press
10 Village Square • Fredonia, NY 14063